D1826222

Kumquat Publishing

PO Box 33632

Westminster CO 80035-0457

www.kumquatpublishing.com

The Dominant Detective and Slandered Submissive

By: Alexandra Noir

Part One: Slandered!

With the photo shoot over, Gwen looked forward to a relaxing dinner with her friend. In her twenty-two years, few unexpected situations had caught her off guard. But all that was about to change.

Wearing a scarf over her light brown wavy hair, she added a touch of mauve lipstick to her full lips and a light coating of mascara to frame her blue eyes. She slid on prescription-style glasses to complete her disguise and set off for the elite seaside Greek restaurant named Ambrosia's. For most of her life, she'd been described with terms like *welcoming, approachable, charismatic, irresistible,* and *ray of sunshine*. While all these sounded wonderful, portraying happiness regardless of her mood could be mentally draining.

Just yesterday, a little boy had run up and hugged her legs. Not that she didn't like boys, but when their unfamiliar noses only reached her belly button and their sticky little hands left chocolate on her expensive skirt...clouds threatened to blot out the sunshine. Tonight, she entered Ambrosia's and gave the hostess her friend's last name. Although the woman didn't light up like a Christmas tree, as some people did in her presence, Gwen caught amusement creep into the hostess' expression. Keeping her head slightly tilted downward, she followed the woman to her friend's table.

"Gwen." Mira stood and kissed the air beside each cheek, then whispered in her ear, "Why didn't you warn me?"

Sitting down, she arched her brow and shrewdly eyed Mira while noting the prompt arrival of their server. When a crisp white-sleeved arm reached over to straighten her perfectly placed silverware, Gwen pointedly asked, "May we have menus, please?" He produced them and waited, forcing her to add, "And a bit of time?"

As soon as he was out of earshot, Gwen noticed a few hard stares from women and highly interested ones from their dates. She ignored them until Mira whispered, "You know I want all the hot details."

Gwen shrugged. "Hot guy and me, beachfront shoot, and the photographer. Nothing new. Oh, and I got sand—"

"Not those details," Mira whispered, frowning as she leaned forward. "The spanky, spanky with a purple whip which everyone wants to purchase now. And who was the badass on the other end of that whip?"

Gwen blinked at her, a blank look on her face, and struggled to comprehend what she was talking about. The server materialized beside her again. Gwen stifled a sigh and pointed to a Caesar salad. "The house ranch dressing on the side, please."

Barely glancing Mira's way, he asked, "And what would you like?"

Mira stared at the man, who was now ogling every inch of Gwen, and said, "A female server whose mind is on her job."

His gaze finally shot to Mira. He muttered a half-assed apology, but outspoken as always, Mira cut him off. "Can we please just get a female server? You're making us uncomfortable."

"Oh, *I'm* making *you* uncomfortable?" the server asked with a snotty tone as his gaze returned to Gwen. "After that sex video, I didn't know comfort was high on your list, *kitten*."

"Se-sex video? What?" Gwen hissed, standing up fast enough to topple her chair if the server hadn't caught it.

A manager rushed over. "Gary, what is the issue here?"

Without waiting for the server to answer, Gwen said, "I'll have you know there is no such…"—her face heated—"*video*! That's a very nasty and rude accusation!"

Their server pulled his phone out, but the manager quickly stopped him from accessing the video in question. "Gary, please go to my office." The entire room had fallen silent. "I'm so sorry, Miss Turisso." Cheeks flushed, he glanced at Mira who had stood as well.

"I believe we need to clear a few things," Mira told the manager and then said to Gwen, "I suggest we get takeout or just order in."

Surrounded by a room full of diners, clinking silverware, and a rich atmosphere of tension and embarrassment, Gwen grabbed her purse and headed for the exit. Mira was directly behind her.

Gwen didn't speak until she was at the water's edge. "What's going on, Mira?"

Usually blunt and proud of her lack of filters, Mira forced herself to proceed with caution. "I haven't seen the video, but it has gone viral. Are you telling me that you're not the woman in it?"

"Th-there is a video?! Oh my God! Of course, it's not me." Gwen slipped her heels off and walked along the ocean's edge. "We need to get back to my room and…" Bile rose in her throat at the thought of even watching such a video. "I need to check my email!"

They hurried back up the beach, ignoring anyone they met or passed. Gwen took the stairs while pulling her hotel key card out. She rushed into her room, tossed her heels aside, and grabbed her laptop. Mira had already searched Gwen's name on her cell.

"Look at this, Gwen." She turned her phone to show an article under a very popular column titled *Getting to know…* Today's feature was Gwen Turisso, underlined by a purple whip.

Gwen gasped and grabbed for the phone, but Mira knew her friend's phone-throwing expression well. She jerked her cell back and cried, "You are not destroying my phone. Look it up on your laptop."

Gwen's gaze followed her friend's phone as if it were a skunk ready to spray its stench all over her life. Mira tucked the phone underneath her leg and opened a tab on Gwen's laptop. Within seconds, Gwen's name along with site hits advertising her worst nightmare marched down the page. Gwen's hand shot up to cover her eyes as her knees buckled.

"Oh…this can't be happening," she cried.

"You didn't get any calls from your agent?" Mira asked, pointing to Gwen's phone which was on the dresser.

"The damn thing died on me, so I left it here to charge." She snatched it off the dresser and almost fainted when the screen lit to show over thirty missed texts and eighteen missed calls. A *TZZZ-TZZZ* pulse synchronized with vibrations flooded from the device as *Mom* flashed repeatedly on her screen. Gwen almost dropped the phone and mistakenly hit the power button.

"Gwen?!" her mother's voice, although muted, was powerful enough to reduce her to tears.

"Mom? It's not me! I-I just—"

"I told you not to go with that agency, Gwen. Now look what happened!" Her mother's shrill voice was the last thing she needed to hear. "And that dolt wouldn't listen to me."

"You talked to—"

"Of course, I spoke to Don. That man is a rude wretch. Fire him already and—"

"No!" Gwen wasn't about to let her overbearing evangelical mother take control of her life. Again. "I'll take care of this, Mom. Do not contact him again."

"Oh, honey, you think you know what's best? The modeling industry will tear you apart, Gwen, which is why you should have stuck with a Christian agency instead of that horrid—"

"Mom, stop!"

A loud snap and a feminine porn-worthy moan flooded from her laptop speakers. Mira stabbed her finger on the mute button at the same time Gwen's mother shrieked, "How did you fall so far from—"

Gwen removed the phone from her ear and said, "Mom, I'm hanging up."

"Who is with—"

Gwen ended the call. Her phone immediately began vibrating again with Don flashing on the screen.

She quickly answered and said, "Don, that's not me in the video. How do I make it go away?"

"Of course it's not you, but it's also not going away. Have you seen this video, Gwen?" he asked.

"No! Mira just told me about it. I don't know what to do, Don, and what do you mean it's not going away?"

"Sweetie, sex sells, especially when your reputation has been so sparkling and wholesome." Don was actually relieved this had happened to Gwen, who was somewhat successful at pulling off an American girl-next-door beauty, but she denied her inner sultriness to do so. "People *love* naughtiness. We can use this for your image even if it's not you in the video."

"Is he nuts?" she thought, but said, "Don, I'm not going to act like that's me in that video."

"That's not what I meant. We need to get together to discuss this with a PR team, not the firm's but one that will tactfully portray you in a more seductive way."

"Oh, no! Mom was right," she groaned.

"Gwen, your mother would have you modeling full length Sunday dresses and demand that you show no ankle. Listen to me. I've had this happen before, and we've successfully dealt with it. Keep your phone nearby. I'll call you when I have something set up." He immediately ended the call.

Near tears, Gwen tossed the phone on the bed and told Mira, "He sounds glad this happened and wants me to meet with a different PR team which will destroy me."

With her jaw hanging slack, Mira stared at the computer screen. Gwen finally reached over and shut her laptop.

"What the hell, girl?" Mira opened the laptop again. "You're trending everywhere, Gwen, so you might want to listen to him." At her friend's scowl, she threw her hands up and explained, "You *were* approaching fame, but this will open the supermodel doors. Whoever did this might have helped you out."

"They need to confess that I'm not the woman in that video." She sat on the bed and finally gave into the temptation to look at the screen. One of the gifs showed the girl

looking directly into the camera and bent over the arm of a sofa with her ass hiked in the air. She was thoroughly enjoying the whip, which repeatedly cracked her ass cheek. Gwen had to admit, other than her lips not being as full and her face being narrower, the girl looked a lot like her.

"Did you watch the whole video?" she asked Mira, who shook her head and clicked on the link advertising the full video. At the first glimpse of the girl, her nipples bulging between wide strips of material that was tightly wrapped around her body, Gwen couldn't force herself to look away. The girl couldn't move her arms. The lens angle backed away, showing her legs spread and bound to a chair and her exposed sex. A blurred head suddenly appeared, blocking her pussy. The girl threw her head back and her chest rose and fell. The blurred head backed away and, in its place, glistening fingers thrust in and out of her.

Although the sound was muted, Gwen could easily imagine the girl's moans and could make out her pleas for more. The blurred head moved upward and stopped at her exposed nipple. Tension in the girl's neck made her muscles stand out for a second the blurred head backed away. Her entire body shivered and then her head fell backward.

Gwen's taut nipples rubbed against her bra with every breath. She'd never watched porn or seen bondage, let alone witness someone who could be her twin have an orgasm. But the activity didn't stop there. She recognized the girl's mouth movement as "*Oh my*

God" before the camera closed in on the man's fingers again. This time, they were embedded in her ass and his thumb was massaging her slit.

"Oh, God!" Gwen blurted out and finally forced her eyes off the screen.

"Damn, that is freaking hot!" Mira said.

Gwen blushed furiously and jumped when her phone rang. It was Don again.

"You are so damn lucky that I'm your agent. Stay put. I'm on my way with a friend and a large pizza. You have to hear her out. Promise me you will not leave the room."

Remembering the restaurant server and everyone's stares, she gave in and said, "I promise."

Ending the call, she heard Mira's gasp. "Damn, he's fucking her in the ass!"

"I can't believe you! Would you shut that crap down before I get sick?" Gwen snapped.

She wasn't fooling Mira, who wanted to call her a prude. Maybe that would get her to watch the rest. Gwen was turned on, but who could blame her? Mira wished she'd just admit it instead of acting like a prude. But she knew Gwen's mother had done a number on her. Maybe Don and whoever he was bringing could convince her to take the stick out of her ass, or rather to allow someone to shove one up it. Mira had to bite her lip to keep from laughing. She really wanted to watch the rest of that video. The man in the video was rocking that girl's world. Mira thought about going to the bathroom with her phone, but a knock sounded on the door.

Gwen answered it, but instead of Don, there was a manila envelope lying on the threshold. She grabbed it and quickly closed the door again. Seconds later, another knock sounded. This time, Gwen looked through the peephole. It was Don and some woman.

She let them inside and pointed to the envelope before Don could introduce the woman. "Someone just left that. I'm getting a bad feeling about this."

"Hi, Gwen, I'm Megan Chan," the woman said as Don upended the envelope, and a flash drive fell out. She held her hand out for the flash drive and asked Gwen, "Don said you haven't watched the video yet?"

Red faced, Gwen glanced at Mira who answered for her, "She just saw a little of the clip that I watched."

"And it's not you?" Megan asked.

"No, I'd never do…*that*." Gwen didn't like the way Megan was studying her, like an exterminator preparing to eradicate vermin from a city block.

"I peeked at your reputation and digital footprint. If you try to distance yourself from this, society will work against you. Your best bet would be to embrace this, and I don't mean claim that you're in the video. I mean that you need to know what you're dealing with so you're prepared to field questions without people thinking it bothers you." Megan held the flash drive up between her thumb and index finger. "You know what they say about protesting too much. Society will turn into a rabid wolf."

Gwen shook her head, unable to imagine going along with it.

"Hear me out. First, I advise you to watch the rest of the video, and then we'll discuss the next step."

"Anyone with half a brain will know that I would never participate in such a thing," Gwen said. "Jesus! My mother is already freaking out."

"Does your mother pay your bills, Gwen?" Don asked. "Does she stand under hot lights with a bikini on and flirt with the camera lens?"

"I get your point, Don, but you don't have to put up with her judgment."

"Yes, I do. She calls me frequently, uses every name in the book, and accuses me of ruining her precious daughter," Don said. "I don't need reminders that she was a top model long ago. The industry is not what it used to be, but your mother seems to think she still has all the answers. Besides speaking with her four times, I just got off the phone with three different clients who want you to represent their products. Your choices are now taking a break, which might result in saying goodbye to your career, or willingly work with us to rebrand yourself. Try out another angle, Gwen, and just roll with a little naughtiness."

"Either path you take, I have just the person in mind to help you. Don's right, though. Choosing to ignore the video or insisting society treat you the same will not turn out good. You have to trust that we have your best interests at heart."

Gwen blushed deeper and turned away to hide it. She couldn't get the girl's blissful expression off her mind. And she wasn't about to watch the rest of it, even though she was more curious than she was willing to admit. She shook her head, denying her own curiosity while saying, "I can't. Ask me anything else, and I'll try to work with you." To take the focus off the video, she asked, "Who are you saying will help me?"

"A friend," Megan said but didn't tell her who. "I can't make you watch the rest of it, but we need to view this. For your own good, I'll let you know a few details. You need to disappear for a short while until everything dies down. Are you willing to do that?"

At Gwen's nod, Megan pulled a laptop out of her shoulder bag and inserted the flash drive. Mira moved closer to Don and Megan, so she could watch, too. With nowhere else to go and completely embarrassed, Gwen intended to do everything in her power to ignore it until Mira said, "Oh, it's just an interview."

A mechanical male voice asked, "So you're a submissive that's into BDSM? Why open up about this now?"

"Yes. I chose to admit this because I recently met a man who asked for me to be his slave. I accepted." The female's voice was a carbon copy of her own.

"Slave?" she muttered and turned toward the screen. The woman was nude and sitting across from the man whose face was pixilated.

"Explain the terms you agreed to," the man said.

"I answer to my Dom, which includes him making decisions about where and for whom I model. He has the right to decline or approve anyone who asks for nude photos. I have relinquished control to him."

"Are you willing to give the name of your Dom?"

"No, he's my master. That's all anyone needs to know," the woman said.

Gwen shook her head and groaned, "This is bad, isn't it?"

"Who will this interview be sent to and why?" the mechanical voice asked.

"My agent who has been advised that any business asking for me to represent them should receive a copy. If he doesn't send them a copy, I will forward one to them."

"Has anyone asked for your representation?"

"Yes, three companies. I'm waiting for verification that they've received a copy of this interview," she answered, looking directly into the camera with a sly smile. "And I'm currently in talks with the maker of the very naughty purple whip used in the video."

"Speaking of which, the video is up next. You should be proud. It's gone viral."

The screen went black. Megan closed the file before the sex video began and said, "We need to find out who is behind this." She then asked Gwen, "Who have you angered in the last few months?"

"Gwen doesn't *anger* anyone. People gravitate to her because she's normally exploding with happiness," Mira pointed out.

"The only person I can think of was the photographer before last, but he apologized afterward," Gwen said.

"Why? What did he do?" Megan asked.

"He wanted me to show more cleavage, and I told him that wasn't in the contract. He copped an attitude, so Shane, the male model, told him we'd stop if he couldn't be professional." Gwen shrugged and added, "In the end, it was no big deal. Like I said, he apologized."

"I'll have my friend check him out," Megan said. "Whoever is behind this obviously has access to your information if they know the companies wanting to represent you. We'll follow up with the maker of the purple whip. In the meantime, you need to lay low and no more telling anyone about your plans or personal information. Gather your things. I'll tell my friend that we're on our way."

"I'm supposed to just stay with someone I don't know?" Gwen asked, shaking her head.

"I'll go with her," Mira offered, "because you can't expect her to blindly trust this friend. I mean, for all we know, Don, you could be the one setting her up."

"As her agent, Mira, my firm loses money because she won't be working for however long this goes on. Even if, by some chance, she comes out on top,

I had nothing to do with this. You got the money to check me out? Have at it."

"Mira, he's helped me in a lot of ways that you don't know about," Gwen said. "I don't think he has anything to do with this. Besides, you're supposed to go to Greece in four days, so you can't go with me." She sighed, frowning as she added, "I'll be okay. Just keep in touch with me."

"What is this friend's name and number?" Mira asked Megan.

"I won't disclose that to anyone but Don and Gwen. If they want to tell you, they can, but I'd advise against it until we know who's doing this," Megan told her, ignoring Mira's scowl. Focusing on Gwen, she said, "Make a list of anything you need that you don't have on you." She disconnected the flash drive and shoved her laptop in her bag. "Do you need help packing?"

"Everything is already packed. We were supposed to leave tomorrow morning." Gwen gave Mira a hug and said, "I'll call you as soon as I get there. Okay?"

Mira nodded, wanting to encourage Gwen to give her the name of this friend, but she held her tongue.

***

As it turned out, Megan didn't drive her to the friend's house. She got a call and said she was needed elsewhere as they were leaving. Don drove Gwen, and told her on the way, "Zack Anson is who you'll be staying with. He's a private investigator who contracts with Megan's firm. Do me a favor and hold off on telling anyone, okay? Even Mira."

"You don't trust Mira?" she asked.

"Right now, I don't trust anyone. Zack is a good PI and, if anyone can uncover who's doing this, he can." He outlined a few cases that the man had helped on. Gwen had to admit, he sounded impressive.

Don pulled into a driveway and stopped in front of a spacious ranch-style home. Based on what Don had said, Gwen had pictured an older man. The guy who walked down the stone steps looked to be only a few years older than her twenty-two years. Gwen had been on photo shoots with less attractive men than this one.

"Don, how's it going?" Zack asked by way of greeting.

Don nodded and introduced Gwen, who plastered a smile on her face and held her hand out.

"Nice to meet you," he politely said and grasped her offered hand.

"Likewise," she said, and tried to ignore the bomb of anxiety exploding in her stomach. She told herself it was just nerves. Zack invited them into his home, and shortly after, Don hugged her goodbye. His departure did nothing to help her anxiety.

"The girl in the video does look a lot like you. Forgive my bluntness." While he spoke, his gaze lowered to her lips, then her breasts, and stopped at her legs before reversing directions. "But you carry yourself in a much more classy way than her."

"Oh, um...thank you," Gwen said, her face heating.

Meeting her in person, she was even more stunning and angelic, a sexy combination packaged in five-feet five-inches of curves and softness. She needed some hardness buried in that softness. Maybe he could tarnish her halo. As she followed him through the house, he thought about the information he'd uncovered. She was definitely unique; a model who was well-liked, polite to a fault, and had no enemies. Time to test her virtue in the only way he knew how; being direct. "Megan told me that you refuse to watch the rest of the sex video. Why?"

He already suspected the answer but how would she handle his bluntness? Her neck and face turned red. "I've never seen porn before, especially perverted porn."

"Well, that goes along with my findings on you," Zack said, which made her crystal blue eyes lock onto his.

"Your findings? Did you investigate me or something?" she asked, her face getting even redder.

"Researching you was necessary. I've seen many actresses and models pull worse stunts to further their careers. If you were that type, I wouldn't have to look further. Needless to say, you're squeaky clean." He smirked as though the very thought bored him senseless.

"Just because I don't manipulate the system doesn't mean I'm *squeaky clean*." Her phone vibrated from inside her purse. She dug it out to find her mother calling. She hit *ignore* and sighed. "My mom is freaking out. If she discovers I'm staying with a strange man, she'll send out a search party."

"Megan will either pull some strings to keep your location a secret or your mother will appear with an exorcist." He made an effort to control his wit by steering the subject back to the video. "I can imagine she was pretty upset to see articles about you being involved in BDSM."

"You obviously know she's very spiritual. Besides, she knows it's not true." Gwen noticed coffee in the coffee pot and asked, "May I have a cup?"

"Sure." When she noticed him preparing a cup without asking how she liked it, she said, "You know a lot about me, but I know nothing about you."

"Ask away, but I may not answer some of them. I wouldn't want to freak you out."

"What do you mean? How would you freak me out?" she asked. Was that his biting wit or was he serious?

"You've already shown distaste about certain things that I may be involved in, but I can forgive your ignorance if you ask nicely," he said. He was used to judgment, but combined with her stellar reputation, her opinion didn't sit well. "You're closed minded. My guess is you get that from your mother."

He deliberately pushed her button. And not in a good way. "I am not closed minded or ignorant, and I do not take after my mother. I obviously made you angry. I won't apologize unless you tell me how I angered you nor will I ask forgiveness until you provide some clarity on the matter."

"You asked for it," he warned. "BDSM is not perverted and distasteful. That opinion shows your ignorance. Granted, the actions in the video were not meant to explain the lifestyle, only to shock people like you, but why not do a little research to understand something before shooting it down?"

"Hold on. Are you saying that you—" The slight smile and challenge that entered his eyes answered her. She went from standing beside the bar stool to abruptly sitting on it. "Okay, why wasn't I told this from the start?"

"Why would you be?" Already sitting across from her, he moved forward slowly as he said, "We only have BDSM in common because someone is bullshitting the public. And, before you start claiming I'm not the PI for the job, let me remind you that, as a Dom, I know a lot about BDSM, so I am the perfect PI for the job."

Dom? she thought, but didn't dare clarify what she thought that meant. He would simply use that as validation of her ignorance.

"Dom as in dominant, like the man in the video. Your expression is very telling, Gwen." He leaned away from her, and as expected, she moved toward him like a flower seeking sunlight. "And so is your body language. You might want to do a little research yourself."

She didn't know how to respond to that statement or to him. Trying to act natural, she meant to say that she didn't need to research anything. Instead, she blurted out, "Research what?"

"How did watching part of the video make you feel, Gwen?" he asked and noted how severely she blushed.

"I didn't pay much attention," she lied, and then promptly asked, "Where am I sleeping?"

He didn't bother pushing for the truth. He already knew it. Standing, he motioned to follow him and led her past his living room and halfway down a hallway.

"Your things are already inside. If you need something," he pointed to the bedroom directly beside hers, "I'll be behind that door."

Once inside her bedroom, she quickly texted Mira to let her know all was well. After a few back and forth responses, which included explaining to Mira that Megan's mystery friend wanted to remain anonymous, Gwen ended by fibbing, "I'm falling asleep. Goodnight."

***

The next morning, Gwen waited as long as she could before stepping out of the bedroom and walking into his kitchen for coffee. The entire night had consisted of their conversation ringing in her mind and robbing her of sleep. She had a Dom sleeping in the next room, someone knowledgeable about how to bind and tease the doppelganger from the video. A breathing and very handsome PI who seemed able to read her like a book and had even advised her to look up information about submissives. Did he think she was submissive? No, she was a novice.

She'd had sex twice in her lifetime. Twice! And she had no clue what all the fuss was about. But that video had made her feel aroused. She'd never felt like that before, not even during sex. She'd thought she was frigid. Did becoming turned on by that video mean she was perverted? Maybe her mother was right. The modeling industry would send her to hell!

"Morning," Zack said from behind her.

She jumped and, in the middle of pouring creamer into her coffee, hit the cup which overturned and dumped the tan liquid all over the counter.

"Oh, I'm so sorry." She grabbed for the paper towels, but his fingers closed over her wrist.

"I've got this. Sit down." His hand slid up her arm, leaving a path of tingly goosebumps as he attempted to direct her out of his way and toward the bar stool. Turning toward him, her view was suddenly filled with bare skin and dark chest hair which her gaze followed downward to his waistband. For a second, her mind was filled with what was beyond that waistband.

"Watch yourself. You're making it hard for me to protect your innocence." His husky tone was all that registered.

"What?" she asked a split-second before her brain grasped what he'd said.

His hand, now resting on her lower back, gently nudged her toward the bar stool. She wanted to run back into the safety of her room. Taking a few deep breaths, she sat with her back to him and quietly listened to him clean up her mess. He finally walked around the bar with a coffee cup in each hand and sat across from her.

"Good morning," he repeated as he slid her cup to her. "Today, we start researching who is behind that video. You are going to help me."

"Okay," she obediently said. "What do we do first?"

"Drink your coffee and wake up. Then you'll shower and meet me in my office."

She nodded and sipped her coffee while he drank half his cup, then drained it. Distance was needed to reduce the sexual tension, which had accelerated from spark to lightning bolt status, as a direct result of her roaming gaze. When he stood and headed for the hallway, she asked, "Do you want me to use the bathroom shower beside the bedroom where I slept?"

"Yes. I'll use my office one. I assumed you'd be more comfortable with the one closest to your belongings." She'd visited the same bathroom, connecting the two bedrooms, four times during the night. He didn't let her know that he'd heard her peek into the shower and explore under the sink to obviously check out his belongings.

"That-that's fine. Thank you."

He nodded and left her to finish her coffee. Today, one way or another, they would reach a better understanding of who was framing her. Zack's theory was that she'd inadvertently pissed someone within the BDSM lifestyle off, but he hadn't ruled out other possibilities like jealousy or a cruel prank. Whatever the reason, the time had also arrived for Gwen to expand her understanding of that lifestyle. Maybe then, she'd recognize anyone with dominant or submissive personality traits. If he was lucky, she'd acknowledge those qualities within herself.

***

After showering, she dressed and applied a bit of makeup before stepping out into the hallway. Then, it hit her. She had no clue where his office was located. Looking to her right, she had a choice of three doors on the same side as her bedroom and two doors on the opposite side of the hall. A set of French doors, located at the end of the hallway, were slightly ajar. Through their glass panels, she spotted Zack in his pool, so she headed outside. Two steps were all she managed before freezing at the sight of a purple whip lying atop a glass patio table. Her mind flew in every direction at the sight, and questions tripped over each other. What was it doing here? Why did he own this specific item? What if he was the one behind the video? While she struggled with rising panic, Zack slipped unnoticed from the pool. By the time he stopped beside her, she'd picked the purple whip up with one hand and was running the fingers of her other hand down the length of it. Her caress, albeit a curious innocence, made Zack instantly hard. She suddenly noticed him and immediately dropped the whip. His hand shot out and grabbed it. He did what came natural with its weight and texture, flicked his wrist backward for a resounding snap. Her crystal blue eyes widened, and a naughty moan underlined, "Oh shit."

From her full pink lips, those simple two words crushed Zach's ability to reason. His hand reversed direction, sending the whip through the air to circle Gwen. He caught the end and pulled both the handle and tip toward him, effectively closing the distance between them. Her hands were already reaching upward to drive her fingers into his wet hair.

Dropping the whip to slide one hand up her back and tangle his fingers in her sun-kissed hair, his mouth closed over hers with every intention of curing his hunger and robbing her innocence. Hard muscle surrounded her, and she was lifted off her feet. With handfuls of his hair and her legs struggling to wrap around his hips, she clung to him as he moved to place her back against the outer wall of his home. When his lips dragged over her cheek, she whimpered from the loss of his teasing tongue.

"You sure you want to take this path," he rasped against her throat.

"Yes, please!" Whatever magic he wielded over her couldn't be ignored. He'd already invaded her sleep and her mind. Now her body demanded his invasion, too.

"You realize you're handing yourself over to a Dom," he needlessly reminded her. "And there will be no turning back."

"I understand." She rubbed herself against his hard cock. Instead of tearing her clothes off like he wanted, he told her to hang onto him before heading inside and taking her to his office. Her clothes joined his dripping swim trunks on the floor. After a moment to admire her naked beauty, he ordered her bend over the arm of the sofa.

"I fuck you now, you're mine," he said, giving her every chance to bail. She wiggled her ass against him and moaned. The flawless skin of her ass cheeks just begged to be marked, and he couldn't resist reddening it a little with a sharp slap. She whimpered and clawed the leather sofa but appeared two heartbeats away from a complete overwhelm of bliss. He tore a condom open, quickly sheathed himself, and ran a hand over his fading hand print on her ass.

Gwen was caught up in a flood of emotions and sensations; anxiety and disbelief taking a backseat to a willingness to do or become whatever he wanted. Her desperate need for him to complete her, take her, to consume her in every way felt like a beast trying to claw its way out of her. His finger explored her as his knee nudged her legs further apart. Almost delirious over the need to connect, she pushed backward into his hand.

"Slick and ready for me and so damn tight," he said, replacing his fingers to tease her slit with the head of his cock.

She greedily pushed backward again, forcing him an inch inside her, and her back arched while she gasped. He grabbed the nape of her neck and pushed her downward. At the same time, he thrust fully into her and groaned at her pussy's tight squeeze.

"Zaaack! Oh my…" she cried.

He pulled back while his fingertips dug into her hips. Struggling for control wasn't something Zack did very often, but her untapped sexy potential as his sub was like a drug. He thrust into her again and slapped her ass when she began to grind into him. "Shiiit!" she screamed, climaxing so hard that he couldn't reign his own control in fast enough.

Gwen felt his cock jerk deep inside her at the same time he cursed. Wild for more of him, she tried to wiggle her ass against him. His hand tightened on her hip, though.

"Oh, please don't stop," she begged.

"We're far from finished. I just claimed you. Next, you will become submissive and learn how to claim me as your Dom. And we'll show each other how much pleasure comes from that connection."

To her dismay, he pulled completely out. Instead of leaving her as she'd expected, he helped her straighten from her bent position and then sat down on the sofa before pulling her into his lap. He cradled her, resting her cheek to his chest, and gliding his fingers down her back while he detailed what they'd do for the rest of the day. Gwen could have stayed curled in his lap forever, peaceful and content. She expected to be shattered repeatedly, just like he'd claimed her, but she'd have to learn to cope with some crushing truths in the days ahead.

Part Two: Threatened!

Zack was going to be so mad at her when he found out that her mother had tracked her down. She'd had to answer her call sooner or later. For two days, she'd stabbed IGNORE on her cell until her mother had texted, "Why are you avoiding my calls? If you don't call me back, I'll report that you're missing to the police and have them go straight to Don."

Her mother never bluffed, so she had called her, but refused to tell her where she was staying. Gwen only mentioned that a friend was helping her out. Zack's name nor his address was said, yet within seconds, her mom announced the street Zack lived on and refused to tell Gwen how she knew. Gwen had begged her not to show up at the house. Of course, she didn't listen. She didn't exactly say she was coming over, but Gwen knew she would.

Gwen had paced back and forth for over thirty minutes while waiting for Zack to come home and praying that her mother wouldn't show up. At the sound of a car, she ran to the front door and peered out the narrow glass panels flanking it.

"Oh, thank God!" It was Zack.

She jerked the door open and ran outside. "Zack, I have to talk—"

His hand shot out, palm toward her, as he said, "You've done enough talking *over the phone*."

How did he find out?

"On the way back, I did some talking, too." He walked by her and didn't stop for his usual greeting or kiss. "My first rule was not to tell anyone where you were and you broke it. Remember what I said about punishment?" She nodded, suddenly feeling sick to her stomach. "In twenty minutes, you will act like there is no connection between us other than your existence in my home while I work. Understood?" At her nod, he added, "You may speak and act normal while she is here, but after she leaves, you will only speak when I give you permission. The same goes for touching me and eye contact. Those crystal blues better be lowered to the floor in my presence."

He needed to know that she didn't tell where they were, but when she opened her mouth, he snapped, "I didn't give you permission. Come to me." Fighting tears, she obeyed, but kept her eyes lowered until he commanded, "Look at me."

Gold flecks were prominent in his hazel eyes, just like when he was aroused, but now anger and disappointment stared back at her. She gritted her teeth, but that didn't stop her body from trying to curl in on itself as a sob escaped.

"I don't enjoy punishing you, but you cannot break the rules." And he couldn't have her looking like the world was ending, either. His mouth lowered to hers, and his lips brushed hers with his next words. "Don't cry, love. When you're sad, like now, I'm sad. Your pleasure gives me pleasure. We'll always be one." He kissed her before adding, "But she won't understand. Our connection and finding out who is doing this to you has to be top priority." As expected, his explanation had calmed her. Since this was her first goof, albeit a significant one, he eased up a little and said, "Tell me what's on your mind."

"I didn't tell her where you lived. She threatened to call—" His phone chirped, alerting him that a car had pulled into his driveway. Gwen spotted it and frowned. Why was a cab instead of her mother's car approaching? When it rounded the slight curve, she saw Mira in the backseat. Zack had already stepped away from her and was approaching the cab.

"Mira? What's going on?" Gwen muttered to herself as she hurried down the steps. She hadn't spoken to her friend since the night she'd arrived at Zack's house.

As soon as Zack opened the car door, Mira flew out of the backseat and hugged Gwen, who asked, "Why aren't you in Greece?"

Still hugging her, Mira answered, "There was some kind of catastrophe so it's been postponed." She stepped back and studied Gwen, then narrowed her eyes. "Oh girl, you've already seen it, haven't you? Why did he let you see it?"

Before Gwen could ask what she meant, Zack said, "Hello, Mira. I'm Zack Anson, and I assure you that I haven't let her see it."

Mira cringed and glanced at him, then back at Gwen. "Well, she doesn't look happy about something. I thought it was—"

"Is there a new video?" Gwen asked, panic rolling in her stomach.

"Yes. With everything happening…" He pointedly looked at Mira. "I didn't get a chance to mention it." Although he was still looking at Mira, he pointed toward Gwen. "You can view it *after* she leaves."

"Well, aren't you a bossy one," Mira said and smiled, showing way too much interest for Gwen's liking.

Zack ignored Mira's attempt at flirting and waved a hand toward the door. "Shall we?"

Mira glanced toward the driveway where the cab was now driving away. "Oh, and a gentleman, too. Thanks for paying for my ride."

"You're welcome." Zack was thinking of Gwen's surprise at seeing Mira. Who had she thought was arriving? And why didn't she know that Mira wasn't in Greece? They had obviously not spoken on the phone, as Mira had claimed, so how did the little liar know where she was? And who was Gwen talking about before her friend had arrived?

Instead of addressing the matter of Mira lying, he walked in step beside Gwen and placed a protective hand on her back. Her friend needed to understand that he wasn't interested in manipulation tactics, empty flirtations, and lying little shits. He lowered his voice and told Gwen, "I'm sorry for misunderstanding who you'd spoken to. Forgive me?"

Gwen nodded and had to bite her lip to keep from shooting him a brilliant smile. His gaze dropped to the lip she'd caught between her teeth. He quickly dropped his hand from her back and opened his front door. Mira eyed him on her way inside, then looked toward Gwen and bluntly asked, "Are you two fucking?"

Gwen spun around, blushing madly, and gaped at her friend. Zack saw an opportunity and took it.

"Do you always create drama to get attention? Strike out for the sake of distracting her?" His tone held confidence that he spoke the truth because he knew she was playing Gwen. And that behavior stopped now. "Lie to get what you want? And demand to know things which are none of your business?"

She stared at him, eyes slowly widening, and then turned just as slowly to show he'd hurt her badly to Gwen. Only, Gwen was now frowning at her. Zack's accusation made a lot of sense.

"Why did you tell him I called you? That I told you where I was?" Gwen asked. "How did you even get his number? What's really happening here, Mira?"

"Are you serious?!" Her friend's hands flew to her hips. "Gwen, you called me yesterday." She dug her phone from her purse. "You said you'd gotten a new phone. So now I'll ask you what the fuck is going on?" Angry now, she pulled up the new number, turned, and jabbed the phone at Zack. "My friend is staying with you who I don't know and neither does she. If you haven't noticed yet, she's very impressionable and I don't want to see her hurt. You can take your opinions and go fuck yourself."

Zack pulled his phone out, meaning to take down the number, but she jerked it away. He shrugged and shook his head. "Gwen was with me all day yesterday. She didn't call anyone from any phone. So, how did you get my number and address?"

With the number still pulled up on her phone, Mira hit SEND and waited, but an automated voice told her the number was no longer in service. She dropped her hand, bringing the phone down, too.

"Gwen, you have to believe me. Whoever is doing this must have called me and acted like you. I don't know how they got his number or address, but I thought it was coming from you."

Gwen didn't know what to believe. She and Mira had experienced a few rocky times over the past few years, and some great times, too. Zack's questions were spot on, though, in too many ways to ignore.

Zack didn't believe her, but, for Gwen's sake, he said, "Whatever the truth is, I'll find it. And if I'm wrong, I'll apologize. Until then, don't expect me to blindly trust anyone." He ignored her attitude and offered, "Why don't you ladies go sit by the pool and I'll grab a bottle of wine and be right—" The alert for his driveway went off again. He pulled his cell out and looked at Gwen.

"Oh my God! That has to be my mother."

"Your mother?!" both Mira and Zack asked. All three of them headed back out the front door while Gwen rushed to explain to him, "She texted me, threatening to send the police after Don if I didn't call her. Then, when I did call her, she somehow figured out the name of your street."

Zack nodded and tried to assure her, "It's okay. More than likely, she has a locator app and found out that way."

"Oh. Sorry, Zack, I never figured that my mother was someone who knew stuff like that existed."

Mira made a rude noise and muttered, "So naive."

Gwen glared at her and shocked Zack when she hissed, "Fuck. You. Bitch."

Mira smirked and waited until her mother's driver door opened, then loudly asked, "What? I must have heard you wrong. Can you repeat that?"

"Knock if off," Zack said through gritted teeth. Then focused on their new issue, who was standing in his driveway with a proudly displayed crucifix necklace. Her expression would shrivel Satan's soul. He almost said *"Welcome to the asylum. Please check your halo at the door."*

"Hello, Ms. Turisso, I'm—"

"A private investigator with whom Gwen should not be sharing alone time." Her cold gaze shifted to Gwen. "I raised you better than this, young lady. Get in the car. You're coming home with me."

"No, I'm not, Mother. I'm not an idiot, and I don't need someone constantly hovering over me. I can think for myself." Not giving her mother a chance to speak, she added, "You should be thanking Zack for helping me find out who's doing this."

"Thank him?" she asked in disbelief. "I'll do no such thing! Do you know what Brother David found out?"

"Mother, your pastor is not a private investigator, no matter what you think. Zack is—"

"A Satan worshiper!"

Zack didn't catch his amused *"Ha"* in time. He had expected mention of his lifestyle. Accusations of being a Satan worshiper were nothing. He glanced at Gwen in time to see her roll her eyes.

"Get in. This car. Now!" her mother said, her face growing red.

Mira's hand shot up to cover her mouth as the laughter she'd been holding in spilled out. Of course, Gwen's mother grew even angrier and pointed a finger at her. "You still hang around with this…tramp! What happened to make you fall so far, Gwen?"

"You happened!" Temper hitting nuclear, Gwen shrieked at her, "You drove Dad and every friend I ever had away, then you drove me away. Now, you'll drive yourself away from me. Just leave. Let me be. I don't need your brand of *help*."

Shock crossed her mother's face for a second before she turned and jerked the door open. "You'll regret this," she shot back and climbed behind the wheel.

Oh wow! The angel has had her wings clipped! Mira thought, trying to stop her laughter which graduated to hysterics. Tears rolled down her cheeks, and she bent over gasping for breath between high-pitched squeals.

She heard Zack, his calm tone underlined with ice, ordering her a cab. Gwen was staring at her with a mixture of hurt and anger.

"How can you find that funny?" she snapped, her voice heavy with emotion.

Zack finished his call and said, "You have to have some pretty negative feelings toward Gwen to act like that. You need to get out of my sight."

"You're always the one who everyone picks. The bright little beautiful angel, batting her blue eyes, who gets all the good shoots." Jealousy flared hot. Mira didn't realize she'd moved toward Gwen until Zack stepped between them. She backed away, but her anger spilled out. "I had to claw and fuck my way to the top, but not you! It's about time someone choked you with your halo."

"You're the one trying to ruin me, aren't you?" Gwen yelled. "Which guy did you hire and who's the girl?"

"I had nothing—"

"Enough!" Zack's voice sliced through the air, silencing her. "You are no longer welcome in my home. You will be investigated, AND the authorities as well as your agent will receive my results. Consider yourself notified."

"I'll sue you!" she threatened.

"Try it." He pointed at one security camera out of several which were mounted along the edge of his roof. "No attorney who values his career will touch you."

Stunned by her vehemence, Gwen shook her head. Their friendship was over. She would never be able to trust anyone in the business again. Tears streamed unchecked down her face as betrayal, loss, and grief set in. Zack reached out and urged her toward the house, leaving Mira alone to wait for the cab.

Zack sat Gwen on the sofa and knelt beside her. "I'm sorry I didn't listen to you. We haven't discussed safe words yet, but you need to choose one that you won't forget. If I turn into the world's worst idiot again, love, yell that damn word as loud as you can. It's meant to wake my stupid ass up in situations like that or if I get too rough during sex."

"Is there a reason you chose to nickname me *love*?" she asked, hoping he'd say something to jar her out this numb state.

"You remind me that love and inner beauty exists. Do you want me to change it?"

"No! Thank you." His explanation was close enough for now. "I was really naive about her, wasn't I?"

"You trusted her and she used it. If naivety is involved, it was her doing." He leaned over and kissed her, then said, "Now, will you help me find out who that bitch really is?"

"Yes." She appreciated him including her and giving her a purpose.

Zack grabbed his laptop and entered Mira's information into every database and site he could access and a few with the help of a 'friend'. Two shoplifting charges, numerous bounced checks, a handful of unpaid speeding, parking, and reckless driving tickets appeared before he hit pay dirt; a list of aliases and Social Security Numbers.

"Oh, fuck! She ruins one identity so she becomes someone else. And I'll bet she wasn't going to Greece. Her passport has probably been flagged."

Gwen pointed at the name Hannah Walters and said, "She told me that was her cousin who's married to some guy named Brent."

"Brent Walters, seventy-six years of age, is deceased. Ooh, is she forging insurance policies and pulling the rug out from under helpless widows?" He held a finger up and grabbed his phone. After jotting down her phone number, he made a call and gave her name to

58

someone. After hanging up, he shook his head and whistled. "He said, and I quote, 'She stuck her head in the wrong guillotine,' and this guy means business."

Gwen winced. "Even though she's trying to ruin me now, I feel like I'm her executioner."

"To be truthful, I'm not sure she's the one behind those videos."

"Really?"

"She could have ruined you by wrecking your reputation in easier ways. Those videos were a lot of work. Too much work for someone who obviously places her energies elsewhere." He ran a finger down her arm and then turned back to his laptop. She had a sinking feeling, which he proved correct with a couple of clicks.

"I need you to watch this." He paused the video and told her, "I get that it'll be weird watching someone who looks like you involved in a sex video and that everyone believes it's you. If you're serious about helping me find out who is behind this, then you need to pay attention. Tell me about anything that looks familiar or grabs your attention."

She ran a hand over her eyes, slid it to her mouth, and then dropped it to her lap. "I need a drink to watch it."

"Deal. Wine or something stronger?"

"Stronger. A strawberry daiquiri sounds good." She looked over at him, and he grinned at her hopeful expression.

"Come help me make a pitcher." He didn't want her sitting there and rolling Mira around in her mind.

She obediently stood and followed him into the kitchen. While they worked, he encouraged her to think of a safe word. After a few tries, one of which was strawberry, he said, "Make it shorter and something memorable. A one-syllable word will be easier to remember."

"Um…fire?" She paused from putting ice in the blender and glanced at him.

"That's more like it."

"But what if there really is a fire?"

"Now, you're over-thinking it." He took over the blender and then poured their drinks. Before he started the video, he said, "I know a few things you like, but we need to push your boundaries a little. What do you fantasize about?"

She'd already drunk enough to feel tipsy which loosened her tongue. "I only started fantasizing after..." She giggled and covered her mouth. "Before meeting you, I thought I was frigid." At his slow smile, she nodded. "I'd only had sex twice before you and both times did nothing for me."

"You mean you hadn't had an orgasm before me?"

Her face heated as she nodded. "Crazy, huh?"

"Hell, that's sexy as fuck. I'm guessing that you've never blown a guy or had anal."

Her nose wrinkled. "No. With you, I'd be willing to taste, but anal? Eww."

"Remember pushing boundaries, love. Keep an open mind. You'll be shocked at what you like." He reached over and clicked the video.

Although he appeared to be watching it, he was really studying her with his peripheral vision. Her hand with the drink had stopped halfway to her mouth which was open slightly. Mesmerized, she gasped when the man moved to show the girl with a ball-gag that had a hole in the middle. She was blindfolded and sitting in a chair. Cream-colored material wrapped around her body, all but her pink nipples, and her legs were spread wide. The same material wound around her lower legs and secured them to the chair. The bindings were similar to the first video, but the crack of a whip could be heard in the background. Each sharp sound, louder and then off in a different direction, drew moans from the girl. Within a few minutes, the whip's end made contact between the girl's legs. She jerked and made a loud garbled noise through the ball-gag.

The man's mechanically treated voice said, "You naughty slut! Try that again, and I'll tear that clit off."

Gwen almost dropped her daiquiri, but managed to set it on the coffee table. The whip struck again, this time hitting a nipple. The girl began panting harshly as the man said in a tone that implied he was smiling, "Did you think I wouldn't find out?"

Zack leaned forward, hoping the man would say *what* he found out. The whip popped her other nipple. Horrified, Gwen's hands flew up to shield her eyes.

Three more strikes landed and the girl started sobbing. Zack even winced and shook his head. "This guy has to be a sadist."

But then the man approached and roughly pulled her forward. The ball-gag was taken off her head.

"No talking. Suck it good, you naughty slut."

Gwen peeked through her fingers. The laptop screen was filled with the girl's mouth wrapped around his cock and his hand clenched into a fist in her hair. On his thigh, the corner of something white went in and out of the frame.

"What is that on him?" Gwen asked.

Zack studied the video and paused it when the image showed the white square. "A bandage of some sort."

"Oh! Oh, a tattoo. Shane, the guy from that shoot I was telling you about, has a tattoo on his thigh."

"What's his last name?" Zack asked, but something was nagging his memory. He couldn't lock onto exactly what the something was, though.

"Wilkins. Shane Wilkins. But he wasn't as muscular as this guy. At least not in real life," she said.

"How long ago did you last see him?" Zack was writing down his name and the location of the bandage.

"About four months ago," she said. "He always seemed so nice."

"Don't let that fool you." He set the notebook down, clicked play on the video, and reached for Gwen.

She eagerly straddled his thighs while asking, "Have you ever whipped someone that hard before?"

"No. I'd like to know what she did. Judging by how she's bound, he's knowledgeable, but she's either too new to remember a safe word or she thinks she deserves it." He tucked one of her stray locks behind her ear. "Does watching her with his cock in her mouth or how she's bound turn you on?"

"Watching her give him head, yes," she admitted, but frowned when trying to describe him. "If he wasn't so…" Gwen didn't have the right words. "What did you call him?"

"A sadist. He sounds like he's enjoying her pain, and she's not exactly into it. Even if she's a masochist—someone whose mind flips the pain into pleasure—he went beyond her mind's abilities. From the first video—" His brain slammed a picture of a bare male hip into his mind. A hip without a tattoo or white bandage.

"What?" Gwen asked, staring at the realization crawling across his face.

He patted her leg, motioning for her to move, and said, "There was no tattoo or white patch on the man in the first video." With a few clicks, he brought up the other video and clicked play. Seconds into it, he stopped it and pointed to the man's thigh. "He might have gotten a new tattoo, but why do that when he knows a very recognizable mark will be on future videos? It doesn't add up."

The man's cock, mid-thrust into the girl's ass, was included in the close-up. *Look away, look away, look away,* whispered through her mind, but the exquisite tingles perking her nipples and robbing her lungs of air kept her eyes on the screen. Her body leaned toward Zack at the same time the video started again.

Her silence had caught his attention. Now he ran his hand up to the back of her neck and curled his fingers around her nape. She shivered and her back arched, pressing her breasts and taut nipples against her t-shirt. His index finger lightly stroked downward over her neck, and her head dropped backwards. Letting moans and begging combined with the man's grunts from the video play on, he laid her back to the sofa. He could have easily carried her into his bedroom, had another round with the whip, and tied her to the bed to fuck her. He had no doubt that she would beg for anal. Although the sight and sound turned her on, he didn't think her body was ready.

"Undress," he ordered, and she hurried to bare herself to him.

He spread her legs, using only a finger on each knee to guide her. Those same fingers glided toward her swollen clit as he said, "Touch your nipples."

She hesitantly raised her hands and covered her breasts.

His fingers stopped as he corrected her movement, "No, I didn't say cover them. Touch *only* your nipples. *Tease* them with your fingers, love. Pleasure yourself."

She'd never touched herself and was still reluctant, but as she obeyed, his fingers slowly continued their journey and left a trail of goosebumps. She blushed at first contact but moaned when the heat of Zack's hand covered her pussy. Her hips curled into his touch, but he didn't move his hand. Instead, he scooted backward on the sofa and lowered his mouth to her leg. The video played on in the background.

His hot breath poured over her skin when he said, "Listen to the whip snap and pinch your nipples hard. Imagine it's from the snap of the whip."

His hand lifted slightly until she did what he said, then instead of replacing his hand, he lowered his mouth and licked around edges of her clit with his tongue. Gasping and squirming, she began to beg, but he moved away to instruct her.

"You're going to follow my directions and give yourself pleasure. If you stop, I stop, too." Zack lowered his mouth closer to her pussy again and said, "Now, slide one hand down and roll your clit with your finger."

With sounds of the girl moaning and begging for more in the background, Gwen's hand left her nipple and traveled over her stomach. He licked her finger a second before it made contact, and when she tensed and stopped, he urged her finger with his tongue. No further movement happened. As he'd told her, no movement from her meant he stopped, too.

"You want to see if you respond to me whipping your pussy, love? A hard tap from my—"

"Fire," she breathed.

He sat up, baffled over why she'd chosen to say the safe word right now. Did she understand the importance of the safe word?

"I'm sorry," she said, and pointed to his laptop, which the girl was now emitting terrified open-mouthed moans from the second video. The first video had ended and the second had automatically restarted.

"Ah-ha. Okay." He shut off the video, picked up his laptop, and said, "Come with me."

He led her into his office and set the video on one end of his desk. Choosing a flash drive, he popped it into the laptop and pulled up a video featuring a well-done porn with all the activities he'd seen her react to so far and then some.

"Now bend over that end of my desk and don't take your eyes off that screen. If you do, there's always the whip."

She bent over but asked, "Are you angry with me?"

"No, this is part of training. I know you're turned on by seeing and hearing the whip's snap. The thought of its bite is scary as it should be, but you still get wet. So it's time to see how wet and what other toys you respond to."

He turned and walked away as the video started. How was he to find out what turned her on if he wasn't in the room with her? She didn't know that his laptop's camera was on and recording her, that his laptop also would display the chosen porn she now watched, or that the entire house was wired for audio and video.

A few minutes in, he watched her lips part as a sub with an anal plug was whipped with a paddle while another male sub beneath her sucked on her clit. It was the first time she'd seen a male sub in action or seen a woman being given oral sex. He grinned when Gwen's hand slid between her legs, and she glanced toward his office door which was closed.

He'd lay money on her getting hotter than hell at the thought of him entering his office with that whip and catching her. Of course, it wouldn't be in the name of punishment, just good old pleasure. His dick throbbed when her low mewling noises filtered through his laptop speakers. She was rubbing that clit now and still focused on the video. He unzipped his pants to release his cock and brought up the camera on his laptop, then prompted her laptop to open a picture-in-picture of his image. She gasped, eyes widening, and jumped.

"Keep that finger on your clit and pluck your nipple with the other hand. Don't come until I'm in the office." He slowly stroked his cock while standing and lifted the laptop with his other hand. While she pleasured herself, he made a pit stop at his bedroom to grab and hide a few toys. Then, he took everything in his office. She was still bent over and panting while she watched the video and struggled to maintain control.

He sat the second laptop to catch an image of her ass, then out of her line of sight, lifted a small anal plug from his goodie bag. Palming it for now, he nudged her knees apart and slid two fingers into her. He opened them as much as her tightness allowed and ignored her pleas.

"Take your finger off your clit, love." He said and, as soon as she did, he began to tease her slit with the anal plug. He brought out lube and squeezed a bit on her ass for his cock which he then transferred onto her asshole. She dragged in a gulp of air and hiked her ass up a bit. He slid his fingers forward and slowly rolled her clit while pulling the plug toward upward and turning it. She shrieked his name and exploded.

Zack quickly switched the plug from her slit to her asshole while she was still in mid climax and began twisting it slowly. At the same time, he thrust his cock deeply into her. She babbled a stream of sounds, half-words, and ended by repeating his name every time he slammed into her. He tugged and tilted the plug to press against her taint as he pulled out and turned it as he reversed direction.

All the while, she watched him ream her ass while fucking her at the same time that the porn video filled the screen. Never in her wildest dreams would she have believed that she would ever let someone do this, let alone that it would drive her so wild. The thought of him removing the plug and actually fucking her ass was terrifying, yet so damn naughty that her arms buckled as every muscle liquified while a haze slipped over her mind.

A paddle momentarily blocked the view of her ass before he popped her. Again and again. Each hit sent a rush of air with a tingling layer of pain, but he suddenly tossed it away, grabbed her hips, and thrust fast and hard. Her pelvic bone collided with the edge of his desk, jarring her and everything on the wooden frame. His hand suddenly pushed her shoulder down, pinning her breasts to the desk's top. She turned her head in time to keep from slamming her face into the surface with every bone-rattling thrust. With her feet dangling above the floor, he let out a long groan as his cock jerked deep inside her. She heard the laptop topple to the carpet on the other side of the desk a second before he cursed.

He popped her ass with his palm. "To be continued." She gasped when he removed himself and the plug at the same time, and then said, "Let's hit the shower."

After they emerged, Zack ordered her to remain nude and meet him in the kitchen. She heard him in his office collecting the toys and laptop while she searched the cupboard and fridge for something fast and easy to make. Her phone rang, but she ignored it. Within a minute, his phone rang. He walked into the kitchen with his phone to his ear, then handed it to her.

"Don was contacted by your mother again. He insists on speaking with you." As she took his phone, he said, "I'll start dinner while you put that fire out."

She nodded and turned her attention to Don who went on a rant about her mother and Mira, who apparently called to bitch him out too.

Gwen finally cut in with, "Don, what do you expect me to do? We're trying to find out who is behind this. Mira lied to everyone, came over to Zack's and tried to start crap, and now she's on your case, too. That's not my—"

Zack plucked the phone out of her hand and put it to his ear. Clueless of the change of listener, but grasping the opportunity that silence afforded him, Don launched into a tirade again. "Try harder! He's a private investigator, for fuck's sake, what's he been—"

"You had me on the phone, you fucking wimp, but you chose to unload your crap on her. Don't you ever talk to her like that again," Zack said, voice deadly calm but tension snapped around him. He still held Gwen protectively against him while he continued, "And what've I been doing? I've been forced to investigate *your* model by the name of…oh wait, Mira is just one of her damn names!" Feeling an angry rumble reverberate from his chest, Gwen leaned back from his embrace. When she saw the rage in Zack's eyes, she tried to step away from him. He pulled her back into his arms and continued, "If you'd done your goddamn job in the first place, that lying, thieving bitch wouldn't be breathing down anyone's neck right now. Tell you what, get your sorry ass over here, and we'll discuss this further."

"Oh, um…damn, Zack, sorry. I'm just really frustrated with this. You're right. I shouldn't have snapped on her. Mira said something about threats and now no one can find—"

Zack interrupted him, "She's not who she claims to be, and now the FBI is involved. You might want to end her contract before they set their sights on you, too. And I'm damn serious; next time you call here, check your shit before you speak to Gwen."

"No problem, man. Let me apologize to her," Don pleaded.

"No need. She's knows you're a dick." He hung up and tossed his phone on the sofa.

"Wow! No one has ever stuck up for me like that," she said and then frowned. "No one has ever talked to me like that, either, except my mother."

His fingers slid into her hair and his hands cupped her head. "You don't need to take that crap from anyone, including your mother. Being nice is great, but sometimes telling someone to fuck off is needed. How did you turn out so nice with a mother like yours?"

"I don't want to be like her," Gwen admitted. "People avoid her like the plague. My father doesn't even contact me anymore because she'd call him and…well, you saw how Don reacted to her nagging."

"So he's done that before? Bitched you out because of her?" he asked.

She winced, telling him all he needed to know, but nodded anyway. He didn't say anything, but vowed to push her buttons. She needed someone to thicken her skin for her own damn good. He'd grown very fond of her, and now realized he'd developed some deep and unmentionable feelings for her. She was so damn innocent, he was compelled to protect her. Always. That one word— always—made his fingers tighten to fists in her hair but, at the same time, she smiled. He silently vowed that no one but him would ever touch a hair on her head. Torn between being gentle and teaching her to take up for herself, he forced one of his fists to drag her head backwards.

"Love, it's time for some serious training."

Part Three: Seduced!

Gwen sat on Zack's deck and thought about the day before. She didn't know what caused his talk about *toughening up,* her need to have *thicker skin.* Hadn't she showed him that she was tough when her mother had dropped by? She wasn't exactly being nice to Don on the phone, either.

She could remember every word, and how physically rough he'd been. His mood hadn't necessarily changed. When asked why he was behaving that way, he'd told her that she needed him to become rougher; that his actions were for her own good.

He had told her, "Stop being nice to everyone, including me, and telling us what you think we want." He wasn't angry when he'd said it, but it still hurt that he hadn't seen her communication with her mother as tough. If he had let her finish talking to Don, maybe she would have shown him her thick skin.

"I need to see you angry enough to cross me," he'd said. "Knock the nice act off and grow some thick skin, Gwen. Until you do, I will push every button to find what makes you mad."

"I'm not always nice," she had told him. "You saw how I reacted to Mira. I wasn't exactly nice to her."

"And when was the last time you told her off like that?" he'd asked. "Always nice, professional, and that's going to make people run right over you. From now on, the only time you're allowed to speak is when you can show me some attitude. If you don't know how, there are plenty of sites to show you. Hell, sit down right there and look up the word *bitch* on YouTube."

"I do have a mother who's a...a bitch," she'd tried to snap at him, but *that word* had come out too softly.

"Sit and repeat after me." He had pointed to the chair.

She had decided to show him attitude by crossing her arms and shaking her head. "No."

A grin had spread over his face, and it wasn't a nice happy grin. It was an *I'm a lion and you sure smell good* grin. His shoulders had squared, and he had slowly walked toward her. She'd backed up faster, but he walked right by her. Minutes later, he had appeared again with the whip.

"As your Dom, I am only going to tell you one more time to sit and repeat after me." He had looked pissed.

She had obeyed and repeated every vulgar word he'd told her. Her cheeks heated now at the memory. And then he'd made her bend over a bar stool and demanded her silent while he handcuffed her hands to the stool's legs. Like nothing had happened, he'd went about fixing dinner. Afterward, he'd silently fed her.

So what was she supposed to do? Slam everything around, even the front door, and act like a bitch? Like her mother?

What good would that do? She shuddered at the thought. What if she couldn't stop being a bitch? She'd turn into her mother.

Hearing a car pull into the driveway, she went back into the house. Zack had gone to a meeting with the same photographer who had wanted her to expose more skin. He had thought maybe the man was in on this somehow.

She met him at the door where he kissed her cheek and whispered in her ear, "Get undressed and on my bed."

Too afraid to disobey, she turned and backtracked toward his bedroom, undressed, and crawled over his thick comforter. Zack entered the room as she was in mid-crawl, ass twitching. With a flick of his wrist, he snapped the whip and barely missed one lovely ass cheek. She shrieked and planted her ass on the comforter.

"Oh no." He shook his head. "Turn over and, every time you hear this whip snap, say, *'Please, Zack, fuck my wet pussy.'*"

She gasped, and barely stopped her hand from flying to her mouth. He grinned, obviously enjoying every uncomfortable moment he was giving her. Where had the man she'd agreed to investigate her issue with gone?

Then she frowned. If she was going to be struck with the whip anyway, maybe she should just fight him. She tensed but asked, "What if I refuse to roll over?"

"Oh, please do," he said, grin widening. That freaking lion look was back. Jesus! He was scaring the hell out of her.

Zack had heard the same thing from the photographer he'd just interviewed, that Gwen was an angel, and he'd done her wrong with the suggestion of showing more skin. Oh no, he had assured Zack, he would never disrespect her again. He had admitted to watching the videos, though, and excused his behavior with *'who hadn't watched them?"*

Now, he watched Gwen flip over onto her stomach. "Raise your ass and get ready to beg me to fuck that wet pussy."

***

In a tiny cabin in Bumfuckyonder, all the action displayed on a computer screen. Zack, with whip in hand, demanded Gwen beg him. The private investigator thought he was so damn smart, but the woman sitting behind the computer knew more than him. She had hacked into his high-tech house like a real pro. Being a wiz at malware, eavesdropping, and shielding her location was simple child's play for her.

Known by many names including Mira, she smiled when a snap on Gwen's ass resulted in a gasp and then Gwen turned to glare at him. Mira clicked the mouse, capturing the glare on Gwen's face.

"Say it or I'll tie you to that bed and pop you harder," Zack threatened her.

"Please, Zack, keep hitting me with the whip," Gwen said, wearing that pleased look Mira hated so much. Gwen added, "Reverse psycholog—"

Zack flipping her onto her back had shut her up. Mira made sure her audio was clicked as Zack said, "You do what I tell you and stop finding ways around learning how to be a bitch."

"I can be a bitch. You saw—"

"A girl pushed into telling her psycho mother off AFTER years of enduring her shit. *That* does not qualify for showing attitude to someone who deserves it." He was now in her face which was red, probably because she knew damn good and well that he was right.

Mira had seen her get run over many times. That's who she was, easy to push around, and nothing Zack did would change it. She was a damn doormat and worked that angelic persona to nauseating levels. It was a shame Zack had caught on to what Mira was doing before she'd had a chance to rob the bitch blind.

"Accuse me of some half-ass bullshit?" Mira asked, her eyes on Zack. "Let's see how you feel when the real footage hits the web AND is sent to your fucked up mother."

Zack crawled off the bed and ordered Gwen not to move. Grabbing his phone, he scrolled though his contacts. "Maybe I'll text a rougher Dom over to fuck you up the ass."

"You wouldn't do that." But Gwen didn't look so sure.

"You don't think so?" He texted to a friend of his, *"Playing a joke on my new sub. Go along with it."*

The Dom texted back, "*Sure. Send me a pic?"*

"He wants to see the asshole he's about to fuck. Bend over."

Her mouth flew open, then she said, "Prove it."

He showed her the request for a pic text. Tears of hurt and betrayal flooded Gwen's eyes, and she shrieked, "Why are you being such a dick?"

"See, love!" He pointed at her. "There's that sexy inner bitch. Now, give me a peek of your tight virginal asshole."

"No!" she yelled, as he slowly moved toward her with a huge grin. She gave him a vicious look—which made Mira's eyes widen—and she snapped, "Stop it, Zack. No one is touching me *there.*"

"Oh, but I insist. You loved that anal plug, so you'll love my cock buried in your ass." Mira gawked at her monitor when he started removing his clothing.

Panicked, Gwen crawled backward toward the headboard. "I don't want you to…Fire!"

"What?!" Mira muttered. "There's no…" Her screen suddenly flickered and a shrill alarm sounded within Zack's home. "Holy shit! His fucking house IS on fire." Her monitor flickered again and then the image went black. "Well, shit!"

***

Zack's cell phone screen turned red and showed a huge black *BREACH*

DETECTED flash repeatedly across it while his shrill alarm pulsed overhead.

"Security compromised," a computerized voice from his cell phone announced, freezing his blood in his veins.

"Damn!" he shouted, grabbing the cell from his bed. "Gwen, get your clothes on and come with me. Fast!"

She rushed to get dressed as his cell phone rang and the shrill beeping shut off as fast as it had started. Zack answered and listened to his security service and then said, "Got it."

He hung up and told Gwen, "Someone hacked my security system and the service detected they also compromised my audio and video capabilities. Sounds like the sons of bitches now want to leak the real deal to the media."

Panic made Gwen freeze. "What?!"

Zack quickly said, "Just get dressed. They've blocked..." Instead of going into details, which he had no time to do, he said, "We'll take care of whatever we can. My security service is damn good.

Hell, they could probably hack the Pentagon with their eyes closed."

"If they're so good, how did someone record us?" she asked, panicking even more over how little she knew of this man. "And were you recording us?"

Gwen's suspicion was noted, but he had no time to explain other than tell her that he hadn't been recording them and to meet him in his office. By the time she reached his office, Zack had his system temporarily blocking all outside interference and Vic, the friend he'd just texted who had worked alongside the security service, was on his way over. He'd also told Vic that this was not a prank, and he'd explain that text later.

She stopped at his open doorway and watched him furiously type while frowning at his screen. She didn't want to go through him threatening to have another Dom do such things to her again. Concentrating on telling him in just the right tone, she said, "We need to talk."

"Yes, we do." He looked up, very proud of her for using that demanding tone and underlining it with cold attitude. "You want to understand why I'm acting this way, right?"

"Yes. And no more threats." Her tone was even colder.

He almost clapped his hands but knew she'd take it the wrong way. Right now, he had no time to tangle with her over this. He had to block whoever was doing this before she was all over the internet instead of her body double.

"No more threats." He didn't add *for now.* "For your protection, Gwen, my home's security has to be repaired, and I have to make sure this video is secure. Finding its source means we might find out who's behind the others. I don't want you or me going live and viral anytime soon, either." Judging by the way she avoided eye contact with him, he knew he'd have to make it up to her. "We'll talk about my reasoning and my behavior after my security rep leaves."

"Someone's coming over? As in…they might see me nude in that video?"

"I won't open the file," he assured her. "It has probably been corrupted already, so whoever is behind this won't be able to use it, either, but I have to make damn sure."

She thrust a hand in her hair. "This was all a mistake. I should have gone home."

"Gwen, I'll take care of this," he said, standing and moving around his desk.

"Don't." She raised a hand, her palm toward him, but he ignored it. "You've done enough."

"Love, you're now showing me that toughness, which everyone needs to see." He finally stopped in front of her. "I had to make you mad to see that you won't become your mother if you stick up for yourself. I'm not sorry that I forced that part of you to the surface, but my intention was not to damage your trust." At an arm's length away from her, he now offered her his hand and softly said,

"I'm sorry if I crossed the line. Forgive me?"

Another alarm sounded, but shut off after a couple of irritating bleeps which he ignored. "Vic, a service rep and a good friend of mine, is pulling up the driveway. He worked on government software, and I'd like to ask you to trust him to help us find out who's doing this."

"If you start acting like that again," she said, forcing all the vulnerability she'd felt when he'd showed her the text requesting that lewd pic to the surface. She held her wrathful tone and was so relieved that her mother's bitchiness wasn't bleeding through. And she embraced her own brand of bitch. "I will cut your damn balls off."

He stepped forward, crowding her so fast, she didn't have time to respond. Her back hit the wall, but instead of further threats or harm, his body pinned her and his lips brushed hers as he said, "Fuck, but that was sexy! Like a lovely angel, eyes blazing, and ready to own my shit. You just graduated my first personal class." He tensed when he

93

heard his front door open. "Goddammit, I forgot Vic has the code."

Hell, he'd sent that damn text claiming he was pranking his sub—who he'd forgotten to mention was identical to…

"Holy…" His friend's rough voice said. Vic stopped behind him. Zack knew by the way Gwen was peering over his shoulder that his friend's eyes were glued to her. "What the holy fuck do you have going on here, man?"

Vic winked at her and grinned wider. She frowned, realizing it was time to let her bitch fly, so she did. Her hand snaked around Zack's neck and into his hair, then she clenched into a fist a bunch in her fingers as hard as she could. "I've got enough man in my hands. And I also have some skank who looks identical trying to ruin me. Keep your winks to yourself."

Zack's hard cock was still plastered against her, so he didn't dare turn around, but damn was her pussy going to get a royal fucking tonight. "Let go of my hair. Now."

She immediately released it and mouthed *sorry.* If Vic wasn't there, he'd have showed her how a sub apologized for that shit. *Later*, he told himself, and forced himself back in control.

"Vic, you really want a black eye?" he pointedly asked.

"They're black enough," Vic shot back, "but if the fist comes from this piece of ass, I'm game."

"*Gwen* is my new sub," Zack said in a hard tone that no one should ignore, which shot Vic's eyebrows upward. He added, "Either respect her or leave now."

She glared at his friend, who slowly nodded, and said, "My apologies, Gwen. About the identical skank, I thought you were"—his gaze darted to Zack— "joking, maybe covering your path."

"No, she wasn't, and we're now trying to find out who is behind this. I've ruled out the identical *skank.*"

Vic nodded. "Yeah, I saw the videos. She's either a damn good actress or that sadistic Dom is in charge of more than her." He pointed to Zack's laptop. "Home said your video and audio was hacked into and a video was in progress when the alert hit. Did you track it?"

So, he's into the BDSM lifestyle too. Gwen kept her thoughts to herself, but craned her neck to see Zack's laptop when he turned it for Vic.

Gwen had no clue what she was seeing, so she asked if they wanted anything to drink. Both told her a beer. She went to get everyone's drinks, all while mulling over this new video business and finding her inner bitch. It had worked with his new friend, so she must be doing something right. And, best of all, Vic didn't give her the same look that everyone gave her mother—toxic bitch ahead!

***

Mira had rebooted her computer twice and still found no trace of her video file on Zack and Gwen. Plus, her computer had crashed twice since then. The first time, she'd tried to gain access to

Zack's security system and had to back out fast. Something was off, but she couldn't pinpoint it. If she could just find that damn file, she could figure out what went wrong.

Her security floodlight blinked on outside, usually not a big deal since she was deep in the woods, but then her computer flashed an image of uniformed men approaching and abruptly crashed. Mira snatched a small throw rug off the floor, uncovering a little hidden cut out in the floor. She slipped through and started running through the maze of tunnels, taking a right and then a sharp left and didn't stop as she entered a cave and immediately dove into its pool.

She swam deep enough to grab a ledge and pull herself through, then guided her body to the left and shot to the surface. A waterfall roared to her right, but she was in the left side of a pool which led onto land. Muscles growing tired, she pulled herself out of the pool and ran as fast as she could for an abandoned farmhouse. After getting scratched by the ground covering and avoiding anything which could sting or bite for countless hundreds of feet, she staggered into the empty and rundown house. She'd used this location once and knew their dogs wouldn't be able to find her after she'd crawled through a pile of rubbish and into another cavern. She barely breathed when she finally made it into her hiding place. There was no doubt in her mind that they would confiscate her computer, and with it crashing before she could get the information, she would have to get another one and another identity...again.

***

With his chin down, Vic's fingers raced across the keyboard, only stopping when his text alert went off. He glanced at it at the same time an email notification popped up. "Aha! Home said the police are at a cabin in Italy. Malware was sent to a member of their cyber security team by the dumb ass!"

"Did they catch the guy?" Zack asked, leaning forward to see his laptop's screen.

"Fucker used an underground tunnel which was somehow connected to a cave. They said she escaped," Vic said, squinting at the screen.

"She? Does this bitch have a bunch of aliases?" Zack asked.

"Yeah, who are you thinking this is?"

"Mira!" Zack breathed. How the hell did she hack his computer? He'd obviously underestimated the cunt.

"Who's Mira?" Vic asked.

"An ex-friend of Gwen's who has more names than the U.S. has states."

"What's up with you and Gwen anyway?" Vic asked him. "Are the two of you exclusive or something?"

"Yep." And here we go with the string of questions.

"You? Come on, man," Vic said. "Don't feed me that bullshit. You're admitting to being tied down to one sub?"

"You know what they say about first times." Zack had hoped to avoid this, but Vic wouldn't let it go.

"Shit, that pussy must be hot!" Vic growled and glanced toward the door. "Is she tied down to you?"

"Yes, Vic, she is," Zack growled, not realizing that Gwen had stopped on the other side when she'd heard her name. She held their second round of beers and strained to hear, but was shocked when Zack said, "Gwen's different. She's innocent, classy, and…" Gwen leaned toward the door. "I care about her more than any of the others. Maybe too much."

"Shit! You finally fell for a sub. Told you…"

The beers in her hands shifted, clinking loudly. Gwen almost dropped them. She quickly pushed open the door and, for cover, she asked, "Did you find the file?"

Now why the hell did she ask Vic instead of me? Zack thought, narrowing his eyes. *That fucker better…*

Gwen glanced up and caught him studying her and frowning. *Does he know I heard them?*

"Oh good. You brought beer," Zack said and reached for one. She took a calming breath and handed them over.

Oh god, why is his friend looking at me like that? Oh jeez, he knows! The file, ask about the file again. "So, are—did you find the video?"

Christ! She almost asked *are you sure?*

"The video is now secure. The police in Italy went to arrest Mira, but she escaped," Zack explained.

"Mira? That lying bitch! She is behind—"

"They only traced her to this new video," Zack corrected her. "Which doesn't mean she's behind the older ones. We have no proof, but they do have her computer and this isn't their first visit to that location. She's slippery as hell, but we already knew that. And we'll found out more soon enough."

"How soon?" Gwen needed closure, something to occupy her time before she went nuts.

Vic tilted his head and raised a shoulder. "She knows her fucking way around some code. Few people can read our shit, let alone plow their way through it. Virtually, she's almost invisible, and she's adapted *from* her real-world skills."

Zack hid his wince and thought, *Leave it to Vic who hated sugar coating anything.*

Gwen's shoulders slumped, and she shook her head. "It has to be her if she's that skilled."

"I didn't see her brand on these videos, though." Even to his own ears, mere words sounded empty. Sure, he could see the similarities, but they were staged. Mira was a different threat, albeit a chameleon of sorts.

"I get it. The video creators are a team. Their goal isn't about stealing money, just tearing down your career. It's personal. That's vicious, harmful, and sneaky but from afar," Vic said. "The bitch from Italy worms her way closer, lures her prey, and strikes like a snake...but alone."

"Exactly," Zack agreed. "Mira saw the prime opportunity to steal from an innocent, but to do that, you have to keep making money. She helped your career, in her own way. The other party has completely different motives; to damage that innocence but did they hope to stop your career or reroute it?"

"I take it you didn't tangle with that sadistic fucker in the videos, so who'd you grace with a smackdown in your recent past?" Vic asked her.

Gwen glanced at Zack who was shaking his head. "No one. Everyone I've spoken to says the same, she was like the angel dropped into an industry full of cattiness and douchebags. There was never any reason to get angry at Gwen because no one wanted to witness the one source of innocence touch corruption."

She slowly took a deep breath while thinking *Maybe someone got jealous? Should I have exerted myself, shown that I wasn't so nice?*

"Which catty bitch got jealous?" Vic asked her, "Did you turn down a date from a douchebag? Who thought you needed to get another career? Did—"

"I didn't date anyone in the industry. I guess you could say I lived vicariously through Mira. And I got along okay with other female models."

Turning briefly to Zack, Vic said, "My usual pay is expected." Then back to Gwen. "Everyone has someone in their life who doesn't agree with something being done or what has happened."

"My mother is the only person, but she disagrees with everyone who doesn't hold her beliefs." Gwen rolled her eyes. "I was already going to Hell in her eyes before any video was released."

Vic studied her for a moment. "Would she stoop this low to save your soul?"

Gwen's scowl should have answered him, but he didn't know her mother, so she added, "And damage her impeccable reputation with such perversions? No! Kidnapping me and marrying me to a preacher would be more along her lines of salvation." She nodded toward Zack. "He's Satan if you haven't been properly informed."

Vic glanced toward his friend, who gave him a mock salute, and said, "So, she's met our dark lord."

Zack flipped him off. "I shalt dock your pay, you lowly minion."

Vic tossed his empty beer bottle in the trash and stood to stretch. "I'll let you go sow some seeds and reap unholiness."

"Wait!" Gwen threw her hands out. "You can't leave now. I thought you were going to help us."

"I am, but there's nothing more I can do about your ex-friend until we get notification from Italy about what's on her computer. If they find anything with you or Zack on it, they'll forward it to

Home's database which I'll pull from. And Zack will send me what he's gathered on the other videos, which I've already watched, and probably know about as much as you do."

Her computer may still have Zack threatening to… Nothing would have hid her deep blush.

"Thanks, Vic. We appreciate your help," Zack told him and stood to walk him to the door. Vic waived him off, reminding him that he had the security code for his front door.

Zack sat beside Gwen, slid his hand up her inner thigh, and leaned over to whisper in her ear, "Meet me halfway?"

"What do you mean?" she asked, trying to resist sliding her ass forward into his fingers which were so close…a mere inch away from where she throbbed. *My pussy,* she mentally corrected and blushed. Riding on that thought, her mind teased a memory of his hard cock pressing her ass against the wall.

His thumb gilded upward, downward, and then backward along her inner thigh. At the same time, he raked his chin over her jawline and dipped down to lightly drag his tongue over her neck.

"We were going to talk," she reminded him while her ass slid downward, chasing his hand which had already repeated the pattern and moved on to another tease.

His palm kneaded her inner thigh, rolling the pads of his fingers tightly against her skin, tempting mercilessly as he said, "Oh, but we are. I hear you're hungry loud and clear, but my voice is not going to fill you."

"I need to say a few things first," she said, forcing herself to freeze. Zack bit back a groan, knowing any order wouldn't correct things between them right now.

Think Fire! he ordered himself, but couldn't keep his voice from showing impatience, "Like what?"

She turned and whispered in his ear, "I care about you, too."

That was not what he'd expected, and rendered him speechless for a moment. *Vic's fucking big mouth.*

"How much did you hear?" was out before he could stop it.

"Enough," she said, "and what I heard made me want to be your sub…in every way. But no more threats. Promise?"

"Fair enough. What would you say to me putting your stay, becoming my sub *in every way*, and the part about threats in writing?"

Now, he'd surprised her, but it was a good surprise. "If you'll include that you'll always stop when I say the safe word."

"Okay, and if I command you to do something, you'll do it. No more tricks like the hair pulling in front of another Dom either."

Gwen crawled in Zack's lap. "He's not… you wouldn't…was he *that* Dom?"

"Yes, but we cleared that up, and I'm going to be transparent here. I told him that I was pranking you." He ran a thumb over her mouth, then pulled her face closer to his. "I would never make you sub for another Dom. You're mine."

She smiled. "Then please fuck me."

He tackled her, turning, so she'd land against his chest and his back would hit the floor. "Get naked." Then, he remembered his security breach. "Wait. There are no cameras in the bathroom. Let's go."

He wanted to rip her clothes off on the way, but waited until they were safe. Scraps of her clothes were strewn across his tile floor. He'd planned on slow and gentle, but that *fuck* crossing her lips had him rock hard and throbbing. He smashed her breasts together, pushed her against the tile wall, and bit her neck.

Gwen's knees buckled as a flush of goosebumps downward and heat built low right above her pussy. She hooked a leg on his hip while realizing he was being gentler. "No spanking? No toys?"

Leaning away from her, he said, "Are you missing them already?" An idea struck him so he turned the shower on. "The water will be my toy. Get in and lie down. Spread your legs wide for me."

He entered, too, and waited until she was situated. A little uncomfortable with her back to the hard tile floor, Gwen watched him remove the shower head and tilt it so the spray hit the tiles between her legs.

"Tug on your nipples."

The spray hit her clit, sending water splashing over her stomach. Gwen's gasp was lost in the noise, but her moan bounced off the tiles. He adjusted the setting to pulse and flicked her clit again. The blast was almost too much to bear, but just a tease of the strong jet slammed her clit. Her palm smacked the wall as her back arched off the hard tile.

"Knees wider," he ordered.

Looking up at him from the floor, controlling and god-like with the fate of her release in his hand, Gwen's opened her legs further. The anticipation for the next burst alone robbed the humid air from her lungs and placed her an inch from begging. His wrist turned, just a rapid flick, and sent a strong needle of water directly onto her swollen clit.

"Oh sh..." she gasped, cutting herself off. Another flick sent the jet onto her leg, robbing her of the intense pleasure, but elevating that sweet anticipation for the next jolt. Gwen's palm slapped the wall again as she squirmed downward toward the water. "Oh, God...please!"

"No, I need to hear that naughty tongue," Zack rumbled above her. He danced the spray over her knee which splashed droplets onto her clit and stomach.

"Shit!" Gwen moaned and was rewarded with a sharp but brief blast. "Please make my pussy wet," she begged, never taking her eyes off his wrist.

The spray struck with such force, she shrieked and twisted under the pinpoint intensity, but then it was gone. "Please, please…again!"

"Say the magic words," he urged. "Beg me to suck your pussy."

The very thought strangled her, and she involuntarily closed her legs and squirmed, needing some movement to relieve the ache. The spray hit and, although her legs were closed, her body still jerked. His wet foot nudged her knees apart.

"Oh, please suck my pussy, please—"

The pulsing blast struck her clit at the same time his toes slid upward and wiggled against her ass.

She barely heard him say, "*Come!*"

"Zaaack! Oh, fuck, fuck!" The gathering force of her climax exploded, but before the spreading waves had a chance to completely subside, Zack had pinned her to the floor. One hand stopped her slide up the slick floor tiles, as the other slid down her body.

"No condoms, love," he said, and stroked a finger over her slit. "Get up and let's finish this between the sheets."

While his mind swarmed with visions of tying her to the bed and fucking her silly, she asked, "When will your system be fixed?"

He grinned as she fluffed her wet hair with a towel. "They have to make sure it isn't corrupted, then Vic has to reset the code."

She nodded and thrust her hands into the robe's sleeves as he opened the door. Both wore plush robes, as they headed toward the bedroom. She led the way while he secretly chose a whip from the closet and tucked it under his robe. When they neared the bed, Zack swept her up and dumped onto it as he dropped the whip where he could easily grab it. Throwing caution to the wind, he pushed her robe up over her legs while grabbing her ankles and pulled her onto his lap so her ass was bared.

"You know what to do to get my cock hard again," he said and leaned over for the whip.

"Fuck me—" she gasped when the many leather tails hung down and brushed her ass cheeks. He dragged them up her back. "What was that again? You want me to do what?"

The whip handle raked the cleft of her ass. He played and teased. "Oh God, are you…are you going to…"

He angled the handle of the whip, just a tease, then slid the moist end firmly back up her cleft. With disbelief in his tone, he said, "I think I've gone deaf. Can you repeat…" One flick of his wrist sent the tails down to crack her ass. "No, you didn't say the magic words."

A crackle of plastic was all the sound his condom task made. She wiggled her ass, hiking it up and exposing her pussy to him. "Oh, shit, that's…"

"Not what I want to hear," he said, his tone hot enough to set fire to the sheets, and brought the whip's tails down again, this time striking across her lower ass and clit.

"How does that feel? Thought it would hurt, didn't you? Want it to hurt?" The ends were bunched and ready, waiting for a slight bump across her clit.

"I want you to…"—he flicked them, hitting perfectly—"fuuuck me!"

The whip went flying over his shoulder as his arm looped under her thighs. He dragged her ass toward her face and licked her clit, then wiggled the tip of his tongue over her slit.

"Oh, ohh, ohhhhhh!" Back down his tongue went to nudge and roll her clit while she wailed his name. Tilting his head, he sucked at it while rocking her ass side to side.

"Oh, suck…oh, fuck…pleease, Zack!" Rock hard now but hell-bent on torturing her before burying himself balls-deep inside her, he licked back down to her slit and stabbed his tongue inside her. He wanted her to come without his permission, so he could show her how seductive and oh-so fun a few whispered threats could be. Then, he'd wake her up and whip that pussy into orgasm all over again, maybe again with his tongue.

And just as his rigid tongue left and lapped at her swollen clit again, she came with a loud cry of, "Zaaaack, fuuuck me!"

He rocked forward on his knees at the same time as he spread her legs and speared her pussy on him, then bumped her until she was gasping for air. By now, the sheets were tangled around Gwen who couldn't seem to stop repeating *fucking fuck me* or something of the sort.

Those very naughty words rolling off her tongue tore his control to shreds, so he struggled to hold back. But goddamn, her pussy was like a hot velvety smothering vice. He pulled out to ream her slit, and she moaned, "Oh no, fuck that pussy! Don't—"

"Goddamn that mouth," he muttered and slammed into her, knocking them both into a climactic rutting tangle of wild release.

He slumped against her with his teeth latched onto her shoulder, and her lips wrapped around a mouthful of pillow. Falling sideways, he dragged her with him and heard her take a much-needed breath. Over her shoulder, he spotted a car pulling down his driveway.

"Gwen, is that your mother's car?"

She jerked and sat up. "Oh shit, Zack! That's her preacher in the car with her."

Part Four: Enlightened!

With a frown and stark disappointment in her eyes, Gwen's mother stared at them. Her uncle, who she hadn't even known was licensed as a preacher, droned on while Gwen fought her rising panic.

So, Mom is ganging up on me. This must be how a cockroach feels when someone aims a stream of bug spray at it.

"Excuse me," Zack cut in. "I appreciate the invitation, but I have to stop you there. We have other pressing matters which demand our immediate attention."

"Yes, we do," Gwen said, and frowned back at her mother. "I will not be leaving here with you or attending your church services and you know why. No disrespect toward you." She glanced at her uncle to make sure he understood that her statement was meant for him, but since he was staring at her mother, she said, "*Brother* Frank, my *soul* is not the problem at the moment."

He cleared his throat as if that was arguable, but she quickly raised her hand. "Please do not debate me. Instead, why not console her?" She pointed at her mother. "Or has her attitude taken everyone beyond that phase?"

"You listen here," her mother snapped, but her uncle stopped the tirade with a hand on her shoulder.

"Gwen," he said in the same lilting voice he must use from the pulpit, "your mother is not only concerned over the state of your soul, but you are also living with a single man, which is not proper in the eyes of our Lord."

"As we've said," Zack emphasized each word, "she is staying here temporarily for her protection and to help me—"

"You are a PI who should not need a woman who dabbles in parading around naked to help you find anyone," her mother shrieked.

"Mom!" Gwen yelled. "Get with the times. You damn well know that I don't dabble or model in the nude. My *career* is doing great and—"

"*Was* doing great, but look where that sinful industry has left you now," her mother said, looking down her nose at Gwen.

"Leave or I will call the police," she said through gritted teeth. "Don't come here again. I'm changing my cell number and my address. You are so damn toxic."

Her mother didn't even cringe as she said, "You just made our point with your filthy mouth."

"Get in your car and drive her mother off the property," Zack told the preacher, but when the man didn't move, Zack snapped, "Now! Or would you like my nine-millimeter Glock in your face?"

Her uncle quickly encouraged her mother to get in the car while Zack tugged Gwen toward his house.

"Well, now we know what happens if I cuss at her, and I cannot believe she brought my uncle with her." Gwen stomped into the house.

"That was your uncle?!" Zack said from behind her. "Next time, introduce me. I threatened to stick a gun in your uncle's face."

"What was I supposed to say? Uncle Frank, meet my Dom?"

"Of course not. They don't have to know you're my sub," Zack said.

Now was not the time for them to start arguing, so he told her, "You stood up for yourself, Gwen. That's important." He heard his cell phone ringing and hurried toward his office to answer it.

Zack swiped his phone's screen to answer the call and asked immediately, "Hey, Vic, is my security system fixed?"

"Home office has it fixed now. The temporary password should be in your email," Vic said. "And I'll need a few names. Can you forward all Gwen's relatives' full names and everyone she was around before staying with you?"

"Sure. I'll send it right away," Zack said. "Did Mira escape them and do you know where she is?"

"They didn't catch her, and the files were corrupted on her computer's hard drive," Vic answered. "I'll forward what they sent me. Maybe since Gwen knows Mira better than any of us, she can help you figure out where she's going next. I'm going to start pulling information on every name when you send them. You might want to warn Gwen that we'll be contacting her relatives who may then contact her."

"I've let her know this isn't going to be fun for anyone, but I will remind her again. Thanks," Zack said and, after a few more questions, he hit the END button.

He found Gwen in the kitchen and gave her the update. Frowning over the request for a list of names, she asked, "Why would he think anyone in my family would do something like this? That's gross."

"It's a matter of searching for pertinent information to rule out anyone near you," he explained. "And, if they've done something gross and stupid, they'll have their time in court for reasoning. Vic is sending me some information that Home put together on Mira and wants you to look at it to see if you can help us find out where she might try to run or hide next."

"Okay, but she's traveled everywhere, so that'll be harder than you think. I've been meaning to ask you—where does Vic mean when he says Home?"

"Vic routinely works with a team which either know Homeland Security personnel or work there themselves," he said.

"Oh! I thought he was talking about an HR office." She couldn't believe Homeland Security was searching for her ex-friend.

"That's what he wants people to think," Zack explained. "It's easier to get people to trust him if he doesn't come right out and announce that he's affiliated with them, so he just calls it Home."

"That makes sense. Are you sure I'm allowed to look at that information?" she asked.

"He's the one who advised you look."

"Okay. I'm starving," she said. "Let's order pizza."

"I have to reboot my security system. Go ahead and call them. The delivery will be a good test to make sure the cameras at the gate respond." He went back into his office to get his laptop and, when he returned to the kitchen, asked her, "Were you serious about changing your number and address?"

"Yes, that's the only way I'm going to get my mother out of my life. I seriously cannot believe she brought Uncle Frank over with her." Holding her cell, she asked, "Why?"

"Do you want me to set you up on my account and order you a new phone?" He glanced up and waited for her to process what he'd just asked.

"Does that mean we're in this for the long haul?" she asked with a slow smile.

"I'll draw up that contract tomorrow if you'd like, but yeah."

"Okay. After *we* draw the contract up. Should I start researching what a sub should expect from a legal standpoint or something?"

"Let's keep this about what you and I want in the bedroom which shouldn't involve legalities. Unless I collar you," he said.

"Collar me?!" She almost dropped her phone at the image of him holding a leash.

"You might want to research subs being collared. By the look on your face, I imagine you're thinking I'm going to buy some furry anal plug and demand you crawl around like my pet." He shook his head. "I may ask you to crawl around with a butt plug, but I'm not into the furry lifestyle."

"Yeah, I need to do some research." With mixed images floating through her mind, Gwen called and ordered the pizza. She had just hit her phone's END button when Zack's computer announced that his security was back online.

"Does that mean you're recording video and audio again?" she asked, looking around his living room. "Where are the cameras anyway?"

"Hidden in the vents, and no, I haven't set them to record anything inside. Only the outside ones are live." He had wanted to enable the inside, but the Mira incident crushed that temptation.

It was late, almost ten o'clock, but with everything happening—Mira on the loose and her mother's visit—he had a feeling sleep would evade them.

"How about some wine with the pizza?" he asked and then added, "I only have your mother's last name here. No uncle is listed. He needs whatever info you can give him like full names and address of ALL your relatives."

She grabbed a pen and paper and jotted down the short list, then handed it to him. Mother, Cathleen Magdalene Turisso; Uncle Michael Franklin Turisso; cousin Franklin Turisso, Jr.; and cousin Elizabeth Lynn Turisso.

"And your father?" he asked.

"Dad's name is Marcus," she said, "but he wouldn't do anything like this. I should probably call him, though, and let him know I'm okay and someone might be investigating him."

"Yeah, you should. I'll open a bottle of wine if you come read what Vic sent us." Zack stood and went into the kitchen while Gwen sat on the sofa and leaned over the laptop.

She tried to focus beyond what he was planning to put in their contract tomorrow, and what she needed to put in it. Then, with her mind torn between calling her father and the contract, the vacancy under the list of relatives for Mira caught her eye.

"This is wrong, Zack. She has a stepmother who she claims is deceased because she hates her, but I've met the woman. That's one of the things we had in common, mothers who insisted on intruding in our business."

"Good! What else?" he asked as he poured the wine.

With her focus totally on the report now, Gwen added, "She lives in Greece, too, which they need to check out." She suddenly sat up straight, stunned at the memory of her mother's visit. "Wait a minute. She called her Mira. That woman is either someone Mira worked with or Mira is really her name."

"Excellent! Do you remember anything else about their conversations? Places they mentioned?" He handed her a glass of wine and asked, "Something a mother and daughter would discuss which seems weird now?"

"Let me think," she said and sipped the wine while trying to remember. "Nothing else comes to mind."

Zack's gate notification went off on his phone, so he grabbed it and checked the app. After a short conversation with the pizza delivery guy, he let him in and went to the door before returning with their order. He sat it beside the laptop and grabbed the plates he'd sat on the counter before they dug into the pizza.

With only a quarter of the bottle left, Gwen started yawning and shook her head. "This will have to wait until tomorrow." She glanced at the time and announced, "It's almost midnight. I'm going to bed."

Zack nodded and kissed her before opening the latest email from Vic, which along with a *thanks for the update,* asked him to recheck Gwen's list of relatives. Since he was now yawning, too, after ditching the wine for some shots of rum and Coke, he sent a quick *talk tomorrow* email and headed to bed.

He collapsed on the covers and was asleep in seconds. The next morning, he awoke to dishes clattering and the smell of coffee. Gwen wasn't in the bed, either. He told himself the first thing he needed to do was pull up his old contract for subs and brainstorm one with her, but she told him that his phone had been buzzing, and he found three texts from Vic. All of them were reminders to ask Gwen about the list of relatives. She assured him that the only other people were her grandparents and both sets were deceased. He sent the text to Vic and received *tell her to call her father* back.

"You know that phone call to your father?" At her nod, he said, "Vic is now saying to call him. After we eat, you should make that call."

"Why? Did he already talk to him?" She hadn't spoken with her father in so long, she didn't how he'd react.

"He didn't say, but it sounded important." Zack pointed to her and asked, "Are you going to give him your new number?"

"That depends on how our conversation goes," she answered. They fell silent as they ate breakfast. Finishing, Gwen picked up her phone and sighed. "Well, here goes."

Zack took their plates into the kitchen while she called, but he heard her leave a message.

She'd be on pins-and-needles until her dad called back, so he encouraged her to sit down with him and look over the contract he had pulled up. Many areas had been designed for the sub to fill in the blank, and he told her, "Just write what you want underneath, and we can add it into the contract."

"Using toys to wake a sub up from sleep?" she asked. "You better have a mug of coffee ready. Why haven't you woken me with toys yet?"

"Too exhausted…so far." He watched her nibble on her bottom lip and turned her head toward him. "You're killing me with those teeth, love. I haven't been marking you either, but keep it up and you'll find teeth marks all over you."

She grinned. "What if I bite you back?"

"I have the perfect ball gag to remedy that problem," he said and pointed to the contract again. "You might want to pay attention to that." He was getting hard just thinking about handcuffing her to the bed and waking her up with a few well-placed snaps of the whip.

She squirmed and bit her bottom lip again. Then, she glanced sideways at him. "How am I supposed to concentrate on this when you're looking like a lion ready to pounce?"

He gave a god-awful rendition of a lion's roar. She giggled and tried to focus again on the contract but finally said, "Can you print it out? I'll jot some notes on it in a little while, but I'd like to try something."

He'd hoped looking over the contract would jar her imagination and result in this exact situation. "Well, you have my attention."

"I saw a list of gags. The ball gags, the ones with a hole in them? Is that for giving blow jobs?"

"There are mouth gags made for that…and I own one." Seeing her breath catch, he picked up her phone and said, "Why don't you call your father back right now, so we can properly discuss the contract and everything involving it later?"

She nodded and slid her finger over the screen to pull up her father's number again. This time, with her sitting so close, Zack heard him answer.

"Dad, it's me. Gwen," She darted a nervous look toward Zack and added, "I'm so sorry I didn't keep in touch, Dad. Mom threw the most—"

"I know she did, Gwen, and that's not your fault. It's ours. She was protecting herself mainly, but since I heard from your private investigator, you need to know a few things."

She went pale. "Like what?"

Zack put his hand on her knee. For the first time, he was glad he'd contacted Vic for help because he now realized he was too close to Gwen. His decisions would be biased and that's precisely why he had made a rule about not messing around with clients. That rule had died a fast death with her.

"There's no simple way to tell you this, Gwen, and I should have reached out when the mess surrounding you went viral, but it still hurts. Honey, your mother was carrying twins. You were the twin that made it, or at least that's what she told everyone. And I've done my own investigating, so I have proof that I'm not the father of that twin. Do you understand what I'm saying?"

"No!" She understood all right, but she refused to believe that he wasn't her father. "You will always be my father no matter what any stupid test says. And what do you mean she told everyone that my—my twin died? Is she alive? "

"I discovered that she didn't want two children," he explained. "And like an idiot, I believed her excuses about why I shouldn't go to the doctor with her. She had a few *accidents* during the pregnancy, so it was easy for me to believe one of them didn't make it.

Later, during a fight, she told me they weren't accidents. She was trying to miscarry. I'm sorry, honey, that your mother has kept this from you. And that's why I haven't kept in touch with you, either."

Stunned, she sat there and stared at the floor. Overhearing everything, Zack couldn't blame her. He suddenly understood why her mother was such a cold bitch. She was eaten up with guilt and was probably suffering from a mental illness, too. And he had a feeling this story about her twin was much deeper. Her father's next words proved him right.

"Wren is her name. She's not dead, but she's certifiably crazy. Your mother left her on the steps of a church, and the baby was put up for adoption. I discovered Mag's lies and confronted her, but I won't go into all that. When I found Wren, she was sixteen and in a psychiatric ward for trying to burn down a foster family's house," her father explained. "I tried to find out if her condition was tied to Mag's many *accidents,* but, since I was a stranger to her, the doctors wouldn't discuss her condition. That's when I insisted on a DNA test and found out I wasn't her father. She was a ward of the state, but I have no idea if she's still in that hospital."

"Holy shit," Gwen muttered, tears streaming down her face. "Why did she do this? Is Mom crazy?"

"Probably, she was never diagnosed," her father said. "I'm sorry you found out this way, but your PI is searching for Wren now. And, honey, what those people are trying to do to you is not your fault either. I knew the rumors weren't true all along."

"Thank you for that, Dad." she said, tears still pouring from her eyes. "I'll be moving soon and changing my number. I'll send you my new one, and I want you to visit me, okay? Will you do that?"

"Yes, honey. Please don't approach your mother with this information. She'll only spin more lies to complicate this mess and that will keep you aggravated and away from the truth." He sighed and added, "She may not even know which sperm donor is your true—"

"I will call you Dad no matter what anyone says!" Gwen couldn't bear to hear him imply that he might not be her biological father. The thought of him wondering all this time if she was truly his child tore her up. At that moment, she hated her mother with a vengeance.

"You will always be my daughter, Gwen. I love you," he said in a gruff voice.

"Love you, too. Do you know anything else about this girl?" she asked him. "Is she still in the U.S.?"

"My last contact was when she was sixteen," he said. "So I don't know where she is now. To be honest, it never occurred to me that she might be the one doing this to you. I guess it makes sense, since you're a model who looks a lot like her, that she would start searching and figure it all out."

"And that's probably another reason why Mom didn't want me to go into modeling," Gwen said as the pieces all fell into place.

"Very good point," he agreed. "Would you keep me posted on what she tells your investigator?"

"Sure and thanks, Dad. I'll be texting my new phone number to you," she said, feeling numb and betrayed, yet an odd sense of satisfaction that they were finally getting somewhere. "And my address. I'm staying with a friend, who is the investigator's partner, so I need to let you go. I'm sure we'll be having a meeting or hearing from him today. I'll call when I learn anything new. "

"You're welcome, honey."

They said their goodbyes and hung up.

"I heard most of it," Zack said, "which is astounding. I've already sent Vic an email, but I can imagine he's questioning someone right now." He pulled her into his arms. "I'm blown away, so I won't even act like I know how you feel, but just remember that we're making progress now."

She nodded against his shoulder. "Can you order another phone for me?"

Fighting to keep from falling apart, she tucked herself beside him and realized that without him, she would have no one but her father and that connection was very tenuous now. She wondered what he'd do if she did fall apart. Too numb to focus on anything now, she simply watched him enter all her information under his cell account and, when he asked if she wanted to keep her phone and just swap out SIM cards, she shrugged. "Do whatever you think is easiest. My dad's number is the only one I'll be keeping besides Don's, and I can't even think about my future in modeling right now."

He kissed her on the forehead. "I imagine it's hard to focus right now, but we need to transfer your bank account to another bank because of Mira."

"Can you just do it?" she asked, fighting another wave of tears.

"Sure. It's okay to cry, love, and don't hesitate to ask me for anything. Okay?"

She nodded and the wall of emotion she'd been trying to keep at bay broke. Her entire body folded on the first sob, and Zack lifted her into his lap. He held her tightly, whispering encouragement to just let it all out. In all his time and through countless subs, he'd never had to deal with this level of care, so he acted on pure instinct. For the next couple of hours, she struggled to come to grips with what she'd discovered. There wasn't much he could add so, for the most part, he just listened. He knew that only time would smooth her misery out and, during that time, everyone would need to redouble their efforts to stop this twin from wreaking more havoc. In the meantime, since Vic was working on the case, he offered, "Why don't we get away from here for a little while? That way, you won't have to worry about anymore unwelcome visits and you might be able to think more clearly."

She nodded, eager to get away from any memory, and asked, "Can we pick up my SIM card and where were you thinking of going?"

"Vic has a nice tract of land which holds a few guest homes that are detached from his main house. One of which has a very nice basement."

"What's so special about it?" she asked.

"Oh, there's a lot to take your mind off everything. You'll see."

***

Two days later, they were settling into a small cottage which could only be reached by a disguised entrance to a path which, in turn, led underground until it stopped at a doorway. The cottage was completely underground but had a back entrance, too, which placed the occupants on a wide sandbar beside a stream. Gwen sat there looking over a birth certificate for Marilyn Comberly, known to her as *"Wren"* who, according to Vic, had been named by the priest who had found her. He was now deceased. A picture, showing a striking resemblance to Gwen who had no doubt that this was the woman in the videos. According to him, her DNA matched that of the sixteen-year-old who Gwen's father tried to visit in the state mental ward. Vic had traced the male in the videos as an actual Dom who had been living in Illinois but, for the last few weeks, was nowhere to be found. They didn't know if Wren had hired him or if she was his actual sub, but Zack thought the first had to be true based on the way she responded to him. No new videos had surfaced.

Zack now stepped out the back entrance and motioned for her to come inside. They'd only arrived that morning, and he'd wanted to prepare the basement, whatever that meant.

"Before we go in here, let me warn you. You've heard of a man cave, right?"

She nodded, so he added, "Well, this is a Dom cave. I'm not going to insist we use anything in it, but you'll get a see what a playroom looks like. I'm open to using it, but I'll let that be your decision."

"Oh, I wasn't expecting that." She really had no idea what to expect, but a Dom's playroom hadn't crossed her mind. "Does Vic use it?"

"He has one in his house," he said and grinned. "This one hasn't been used in years, but I've thoroughly cleaned it just in case."

She followed him down the steps and stopped at what looked to be a cushioned table in a doctor's office, but this one had leather straps and rings bolted down the sides and chains dangling from them.

"Is that a torture gurney?" she asked, meaning it to be a joke, but he shrugged.

"Depends on what turns the couple on." He pointed toward a door. "There's a hot tub and full shower in there."

"A hot tub sounds nice, but does it include handcuffs?" she tried to joke again.

"They're upstairs in my gear chest along with that mouth gag you were asking about, and the unsigned contract. Ready to sign it yet?"

She hadn't meant to stall on him, but she was a little confused about being his sub now. Discovering the twin she'd thought had died at birth was now very much alive and either acting as a sub or actually in the lifestyle was a turn off. On the other hand, she had feelings for Zack and liked the thought of him being her Dom. Reading the contract and seeing his willingness to accommodate her, toning down his prior orders for her to *toughen up,* showed he cared about her, too. They'd discussed it and agreed not to do anything until she signed the contract.

And now that Vic's previous revelation about Zack falling for her had sunk into her mind, she'd gone from being thrilled and telling him how she'd felt to being scared that she'd told him she cared. This contract made everything hit home. Was she ready for this?

Zack had been so patient with her, and she was thanking him by being moody and confused.

"Show me around here first," she said while thinking, *"maybe it'll jar my arousal into life again."*

She stepped into the room and looked around at the array of bamboo canes, whips, chains, gags, and an assortment of foreign items. Leather straps hung from a chain, multiple loops at the end of some straps, and all of it dangling from a chain in the corner.

"A swinging chair," Zack explained and pointed to a few metal rings mounted in the ceiling, "which can be moved around the room for easier usage." He motioned toward a huge fridge. "For food fetishes and a few other toys."

"Do you have any fetishes like food?" she asked.

"I like using food, but I wouldn't call it a fetish. My thing is more along the lines of biting and catching a sub by surprise which is why I'd love to wake you up...after you sign the contract."

Looking over at the swing again, she asked him, "Do you really think she's into this lifestyle or is she just trying to damage my life?"

"I think she's jealous that your mother rejected her at birth, so she's trying to convince everyone, including herself, that she's actually you. I don't want you dwelling on this, Gwen. Like your father said, the woman is unstable." He held a hand out to her. "Don't let her decisions, fake or not, dictate what you do with me. You know that I hold your feelings— what you *want and need*—as my top priority."

She took his hand and said, "Let's go sign that contract."

Together they went back upstairs, and she actually felt relieved and an overwhelming feeling of coming home after signing it.

Although Gwen slept in lingerie which could easily be removed, Zack didn't wake her up for the next few nights. He kept his hands off her other than holding her on the edge of the hot tub, dominating her around a bit, and bringing her to climax on the night she signed the contract. His mind remained on when and what he'd do. To wear her out, so he could wake her when he was ready, he engaged her in a raucous slashing pool fight at Vic's and then fed her a heavy meal.

Four nights after signing the contract, his plan to wake her up had arrived. Waiting until her breathing evened out and her entire body relaxed into slumber, he slipped from the bed and retrieved a bundle of black scarves. He took his time securing each scarf to folded-down rings which were bolted to each corner of the bed, then attached fur-lined wide leather cuffs to each ankle and wrist. He'd been quiet as a mouse, so she hadn't moved an inch.

Next, he stretched the back elastic strap of a blindfold and gently slipped it over her eyes. He had the mouth gag, which kept her jaw open, close at hand but waited to place it, so he didn't wake her up.

He laid a small butterfly-shaped vibrator lightly over her pussy and then used another scarf to loop through the left leg strap of the vibrator, and slowly worked the material around and under her leg, then crossed over to do the same to her right leg. The result was an infinity symbol to hold the toy in place, but he made sure it would tease her without inducing an orgasm.

Then he turned it on low and moved to sit in a chair, hidden within shadows to watch her from the corner. Her breathing accelerated slightly before her ass curled in an attempt to deepen the pleasure from the butterfly. He alternated between solid vibration to a pulsating vibration while turning the power up slowly. Her ass squirmed, and she muttered his name as she tried to pull her hand down to her face.

"Mmm…higher," she moaned as her senses came alive.

"That little vibration is all you're getting for now," he said as he stood and went to the mouth gag which he'd placed on the bedside table and told her, "You're about to learn how my taste, my scent, and the feel of my cock will drive *you* wild." He sat on the side of the bed.

"Don't think about whether you're doing it right, pleasing me, or anything of the sort. *Your pleasure* and learning to use that pleasure will satisfy me. I will not remove your blindfold or bindings. I will not turn this vibrator up. Only when you can do nothing more than lie whimpering from my taste and scent," his voice dropped to a dominating whisper, "which has your pussy painfully throbbing for my cock, will I remove the mouth gag. And then you may beg me to fuck you in the naughtiest of ways. Do you have any questions?"

"Can I come while you're in my mouth?" she asked.

"No, and if you do, I stop immediately for the next eight days. You have power to stop yourself. Use it. Now, open your mouth."

Gwen did as he said and had no clue how she was supposed to stop a climax. Or even if she'd get turned on enough to have to stop one. Did women really orgasm when giving a man a blow job?

Blinded and eager to find out, she caught his male scent first and the muscles in her back and lower stomach tightened. Rich and wielding a power she'd never imagined, she poked her tongue forward for a taste at the same time Zack slid his cock over her lips. His smooth hot cock ran along the tip of her tongue until she moaned long and loud when his musky aroma surrounded and pitched her arousal into another level. Already throbbing, she wiggled her ass and whimpered. Zack lifted her head and angled her mouth to the side, so she didn't choke on her saliva. With his fist balled in her hair, he slowly slid his cock into her mouth.

Her tongue darted and tapped the smooth surface as she struggled with her growing ache. Each time he pulled out and teased the head of his cock across her tongue, she tasted his pre-cum and felt his bulbous head smooth head swell.

Zack increased the motion, sliding in and out faster and with longer strokes but never so far as to choke her. On every forward glide across her tongue, her back arched, and she whimpered as he withdrew. Her arousal quickly grew, overwhelming her mind, so she reveled in his erogenous musk and tried to taste even more of him. He teased her, pulling out to hover his shaft and balls within reach of her tongue while his fingertips played lightly over her skin but never venturing onto her nipples or below her waist.

Her hips curled upward, seeking more vibration from the butterfly resting above her clit, but Zack had lowered it to a muted hum. Her fingertips ached with the need to touch him and, although her fingers briefly closed around the scarves and then straightened as she twisted towards him, the soft cloth only made her want his smooth warm skin against her even more. From the way her stomach quivered and goosebumps covered her skin, Zack knew she was oh-so-close to melting into an erotic fog. Before he slid himself back into her mouth, he removed the gag and smiled when she cursed and greedily searched for him.

Gwen closed her mouth around him, loving how hard and smooth he felt, and stroked his shaft with her tongue before sucking him. But Zack only allowed her to taste him for mere seconds. She whimpered and gasped at the loss, then felt one hand cup her jaw while the other clenched into a fist in her hair. For several minutes, Zack fucked her mouth in quick short strokes which rolled a ball of arousal, spreading tingles through her and creating an ache deep inside her.

Sweet lethargy robbed the strength from her muscles and left her in a heavy haze of lust. Hanging on the edge of surrender, she fought like mad to maintain control. When she thought the waves would drag her under, he suddenly pulled out of her mouth and only took a second for a condom before thrusting deep inside her.

"Zaaack!" she shrieked before bliss slammed through her and shattered every thought.

He fucked her hard while moving the butterfly vibrator downward and holding it over her clit. She bucked under him, grinding wildly and panting his name repeatedly.

Over the next fifteen minutes or so, another climax built until she went from mumbling nonsense to a control shattering, "Oh God, I can still taste you, Zack." He maintained control until she moaned, "You fuck me so good."

She dragged him over the edge with her. He lowered his mouth to the side of her breast and bit her as his cock thumped her deep inside.

"Damn, I could bite every inch of you," he said through gritted teeth. "And maybe I will in a little while."

He pulled out and tossed the condom in the trashcan, then took her blindfold off and freed her from the restraints.

"Don't move yet. Your shoulders will be a little sore," he explained and gently massaged them. "How's that feel?"

"Better." With his help, she rolled onto her side, so he could spoon her. Zack's plan to move them into the shower went south when they fell asleep in less than twenty minutes. His last thoughts were centered on arranging her in the hanging chair in the basement, so she could enjoy another round of tasting him. Of course, he had no idea that their near future included all sorts of shit hitting the proverbial fan.

Part Five: Dominated!

Gwen closed her laptop, leaned against Zack, and suggested, "I want you to dominate me."

"Well, that's a relief since I am your Dom," he shot back.

Grinning at his sarcasm, she slid sideways on the sofa and swung her leg over his to straddle his thighs. "You've never asked me to kneel for you, avoid looking directly at you, or stuff like that."

"Seeing pleasure in your eyes pleases me, Gwen, and everything you read about BDSM doesn't apply to every couple. Does the thought of displaying yourself or kneeling in any position turn *you* on?"

"The thought doesn't," she admitted, "but I wasn't sure if you were just avoiding that style because I'm new."

"I have adjusted some because you're new, and because you've been in a discovery process lately. My patience doesn't mean you're not pleasing me. Okay?"

"Thank you for being patient," she said and kissed him. "There are so many aspects to this lifestyle, and I guess I'm getting a little confused."

"What's confusing you?" he asked.

"About the videos," she said and then tried to figure out how to explain her confusion.

"Are you worried because we don't act like some couples do? Or is this more along the lines of what you've seen in Wren's videos?" he asked.

"Yeah, about those. The guy always has her tied up," she said, frowning because she really didn't want to be tied up all the time, but did that make her a rebellious sub? Or was Zack not into tying her up?

He slid a hand up her back and pulled her in for a long kiss, then said, "Go downstairs, and I'll tie you up if you'd like."

"It's not that. I like how we play, but…" She looked at him, trying to read his expression, "Is it enough for you?"

"I'd let you know if it wasn't enough." Zack patted her ass and added, "Seriously, go downstairs and get ready for me. I think it's time we used that swinging chair, and I have a few ideas I'm sure you'll like on how."

"Okay." She scrambled off his lap and hurried downstairs. Moments later, he joined her and ordered, "Sit in the seat and don't squirm."

She gingerly sat down and he helped her secure the shoulder harness and told her, "Your feet go through these loops and you'll hold on to the ones now dangling in front of you."

Smiling in anticipation, she did as he directed and was soon hanging with her legs spread and her hands gripping the two dangling loops in front of her. She saw him walk away and frowned before low music filled the air. She strained to watch to see where he went, but the chair turned too slowly for her to catch his movement. When he returned to her, he was holding a dildo.

Her eyes widened. "Oh, you're not—"

"Play first, then fuck," he said.

"But I wanted to *fuck* now," she purred.

He pulled a ball gag out of his pocket and quickly shoved it in her mouth, securing Velcro at the back while saying, "My wish, my command, and let's play a game. I'll be watching you *finger yourself* while *you* use this dildo to fuck your pussy and both our minds." He grinned when her eyes widened even more. "See how pleasurable that sounds? Make that pleasure real and I'll fuck you silly."

She tried to grin, but only her cheeks plumped and her eyes smiled. She almost bit through the gag when the dildo stroked across her asshole, but he didn't insert it in *that* hole. She relaxed until he teased her slit and pushed its wide girth inside her.

After sitting on the sofa, he turned the vibrating dildo on so the inner beads would roll clockwise from the base of the dildo and climb upward towards its head. At the same time, the toy sent a swirling pulse along its length so that it mimicked a live cock fucking her. He kept the same speed and pulse strength for a while, watching her body tense, her skin pimple with goose bumps, and sweat break out on her face. "That dildo is strapped to you so that when you open your legs wider, it goes deeper. Close your legs and it will withdraw. Now, hold those dangling loops with one hand and finger your pussy with the other."

"Mmmmm," Gwen grunted around the ball gag and carefully transferred both loops to her left hand. Seeing that she wasn't going to topple backwards and kill herself, she reached down and touched herself. The sensation mixed with the vibration made her involuntarily close her legs. As he'd said, the dildo slid outward.

She groaned again and lightly touched her clit while opening her legs. With her eyes on Zack the entire time, she didn't miss his attentive and heated look. She closed her legs again, realizing the movement shot pleasure through her and made him focus even more.

Her legs opened a little, and he groaned when she dragged her finger over the dildo and up onto her clit. Down again and up, then circling her glistening little pearl. Her breathing grew harsh. The vibrator's inner beads increased in speed and its pulse grew stronger, but Zack didn't let her know that he held control of the remote. She closed her legs, but her finger sank deeper and returned with an enticing slickness, then stopped. He glanced up and saw challenge in her eyes, but she was on the verge of succumbing to desire. Out of his peripheral vision, he saw her hand move downward and her legs inch opened but stop a second before desire won the battle. Her head fell back, and she whimpered.

He hadn't told her not to climax. On the contrary, he wanted her to blow her mind and his along with it as many times as she could. She tried to hold back and struggled to keep her legs from opening further, but when her back arched in the swing, her legs had nothing to brace against.

When they spread, the dildo sank deeper into her and revealed her finger lightly pressing over her clit. But that was all it took.

She jerked and mewled against the gag, then opened her legs as wide as they would spread and curled her hips to greedily fuck herself. For a brief moment, Zack was tempted to force her legs wider while kneeling to bite her inner thigh. But he was having too much watching her now try to grind her hips and engulf the dildo.

She suddenly lifted her head, begging him with her eyes, but he simply grinned and shook his head while saying, "More."

She forced her legs closed and emitted a frustrated sound around the gag. Then, they both froze when a knock sounded from upstairs.

"Stay put. I'll be right back," he told her and then chuckled because she was strapped into the chair. She couldn't go anywhere unless he released her.

He rushed upstairs, pulling his shirt out of his jeans on the way to cover his cock, and opened the front door.

Vic held up a report, at least five sheets of paper, and asked, "Do you guys have a minute or should I come back in a bit?"

"Leave that here and give us a minute," Zack said, taking the report and adding as he closed the door, "I'll text you after we read it."

He heard Vic's positive answer through the door before he retraced his steps and told Gwen, "We'll finish later."

He removed everything and unstrapped her from the chair. She staggered for a moment before sitting down on the sofa. "We have got to get one of those chairs. What's so—"

He held up the report. "Vic just dropped it off. I told him we'd text him after we read it, and I have a funny feeling we're going to need some booze."

She dressed as quickly as she could and went upstairs to find him pouring soda into two tumblers of whiskey.

She started reading, but the information wasn't what she expected. Her mind was also still craving the chair. She accepted the drink and poured half of it down her throat before the words 'Mira's hard drive' grabbed her attention.

"Listen to this," she told Zack. "The Italian police force found files on Mira's hard drive, but they didn't amount to much. They've been wiped from her hard drive. The web has been searched using top-notch technology, including facial recognition software, but no trace of videos was found." She put a hand on her chest and said, "That's a relief! But I hate that she's still on the loose."

Zack held a hand out for the report. "Are you sure? There's at least five pages here, and there's print on the front and back of every one of them."

He skimmed and stopped at several places, but didn't tell Gwen what he'd stopped on, before continuing to search for Mira's name.

"Here we go! Page four reads, 'After an extensive search, the woman known as Mira was located purely by chance in the private dwelling of an older female—name withheld—who claimed to be her mother. The Italian police located this person of interest after a string of elderly patients died under the care of a nurse only to find that said nurse's identity had been stolen. The woman of interest, masquerading as Mira's mother, was apprehended along with Mira. Both were charged with murder, attempted murder, fraud, identity theft...'"

Zack stopped reading and looked up at Gwen. "Sorry, love."

Gwen sat, wide-eyed and too stunned to talk, as she tried to cope with the knowledge that she'd visited with these two ruthless thieving murderers.

"I'm texting Vic because I'm sure we're going to have questions," he said, already preparing the text. He'd skimmed through more shocking information, so he had plenty of questions. "Are you okay?"

"Zack, I hung out with not one but two murderers." Her entire body shuddered.

He pushed the Jack and Coke towards her. "You had no way of knowing, and because she was jealous of you, she was caught and so was the woman claiming to be her mother. You helped them catch Mira."

Gwen drained the glass and poured more whiskey into the tumbler. She'd heard the 'by chance' part but didn't argue with him. Vic's knock at the door jolted every inch of her.

At Zack's call of "Enter," Vic joined them in the kitchen and asked, "How much did you read?"

"She only knows the parts about Mira," Zack told him. Vic groaned as he grabbed a tumbler for his own share of whiskey.

"Do you want me to summarize or would you rather just start asking questions?" he asked Zack.

"I skimmed it, so a summary will do. We need to work through this." He shot his partner a take-it-slow look.

"Gotcha. Okay, so we know that there are two Doms involved with your twin." Vic waited for questions, but Gwen only took a drink while Zack urged him to keep going.

"We know who one of them is, but not the other. We're still in research phase on the other. You know they have Mira. She had nothing to do with your twin or the two Doms, Gwen." She nodded her understanding and waited.

"They were unable to connect the Dom who's been identified to you in any way, so we think she just hired someone." He glanced at Zack. "Did you read…uh, what comes next?"

"Yeah." Zack held up a finger as he downed his drink. Death was not a matter he liked discussing with anyone. "The Dom he's talking about was found in a marshy area in Louisiana. He appears to have lost a fight with a gator."

"I'm afraid to ask," Gwen said and, even though she knew the answer, she asked anyway, "Is-is he dead?"

"Yeah. He was drugged and dumped. They found him near a marsh. Water was discovered in his lungs and signs of a brutal fight. He wasn't completely intact, but he also wasn't in the water." Vic stopped detailing when Zack pointedly cleared his throat.

"That's horrible!" Gwen said and shuddered again.

"So how do you know we're dealing with two Doms?" Zack asked.

"A flash drive found on the body showed an extended version of the last video. Two male voices were present, and both acted as Doms. We also found that, in one of the videos, there was a bandage on the male's thigh and the surrounding skin had been shaved which points to a tattoo. The one found had no tattoos or work done to remove a tattoo on either of his thighs."

"Has Wren been located?" Gwen asked.

"No, we're still tracking everything the one Dom was connected to—motels, background checks, residences, his job—and no one has seen Wren with him. Most have heard about the videos, but that's their only knowledge of the girl."

Gwen's phone buzzed in her pocket. She took it out and said, "I have to give my new number to Don. He just emailed me and said he's trying to reach me by phone."

"Just let him know you'll give everyone your new number after this investigation is over," Zack said. He didn't think Don would give out her number, but he'd rather keep everything simple for now. "He'll just have to be happy with your contact through email."

"Okay, back to the report," Vic said. "Other than the two videos on the flash drive, nothing else was on it. The police are searching the crime scene, but they haven't found fingerprints or anything to suggest he fought the other Dom. My best guess is that he may be a bisexual switch." He glanced at Gwen, ready to explain.

"I know what that means," she said, "but I don't get the significance."

"Would Wren hire a bisexual switch and why? To muddle things and confuse everyone?" Vic asked and then suggested, "Or is someone else doing the hiring?"

"She's just jealous and wants to ruin me. Do you really think someone else is behind this?" Gwen asked, already shaking her head.

"We're searching every possibility, Gwen, that's all I'm saying," Vic told her.

Her phone buzzed again, so she pulled it out and saw another notification from Don. She asked Vic if there was anything else from the report, and he shook his head. "Let me email him before he drives me nuts." When she pulled the email up, she didn't expect to find a modeling offer from a well-known makeup establishment. "Oh, Jesus! Why now?" she said as sent the same exact words back to him. He immediately responded with an offer she'd be crazy to refuse. Her pay would be double and the manufacturer wanted to use the current situation in their commercial by altering her appearance with their product before stripping it away.

She handed her phone to Zack whose eyes widened. She clasped her hands under her chin and asked, "Can I please do this? You can come with me. I mean, it's just makeup and headshots which will show viewers how easy it is to fool everyone. It's a win-win for everyone and I get paid every time it airs."

"I'll put a spy app on your phone that runs in the background, records audio and video, and traces wherever you are."

Vic quickly pointed out, "An issue with that is, if she is in danger, her phone will be the first thing to be destroyed."

"Wow, guys, way to bum me out. Do you really think Don is a danger?"

"At this point, everyone is a danger," Vic said and motioned toward the report, "because someone has been killed. If this is a *real* commercial, I'm thrilled for you. Until then, I'm skeptical."

"Tell Don they'll have to pay me for security and not to leak your presence to the public," Zack said, "but don't mention anything else. If he okays those conditions right away, he's not checking with any company."

Gwen nodded and quickly sent the information back to Don whose reply made her grin and announce, "He'll check and get back in touch by tomorrow at the latest."

While she was working, Vic and Zack talked about the exact areas and details of the investigation. By the time Vic left, they'd finalized a plan for everything from her security to what was on the menu for that night's dinner.

Relieved that she was now getting back into a familiar zone, the night flew by for Gwen. After dinner, Zack ordered her back into the basement and strapped her into the chair again with the same dildo, ball gag, and directions. This time, though, he commanded, "Show me how bad you want me by obeying every word I say. Eye contact is a must. If you look anywhere but my eyes, you'll only be prolonging your time in that chair, and I'll turn down the power to that dildo. If you disobey me, this game is over. Understand?"

She nodded, never looking away from his eyes. He then shed his clothes, but left his boxers on to entice her. She was already fighting the temptation to look at his cock. He turned the dildo on and sat with his legs slightly spread, cock already hard and jumping slightly against his tight boxers. She dragged in a harsh breath and her eyes glazed but stayed focused on his.

"Work those legs slowly to show me how you'd pleasure yourself," he ordered, daring her with his eyes to disobey while his commanding tone made her moan.

"I'll tell you when I want to hear you. Feed me your pleasure through your sight, not your voice," Zack directed and slid his hand down to stroke his cock. "Touch yourself like I'm doing."

Gwen resisted looking down at his hand, only relying on her peripheral vision to see him slowly running his fingers down his shaft. She grabbed both loops in her left hand, trying to breathe evenly and obey him, and then slid her right one down to stroke herself.

"Slower with your finger and widen those lovely legs." His voice had gone to a smooth deep tone which she felt over her skin like soft suede wrapping around her. "Deeper, love." He leaned forward while spreading his own legs, taking the angle of her line of sight down so that one small movement would zero her sights on his hard cock. He suddenly straightened. Her eyes betrayed her, flitting downward for a greedy peek before jerking back up to meet his.

"Oh no," he dragged the words out, deep and smooth, while wagging the remote in the air as he turned the vibration down to a low hum. Spread fully with her finger moving slowly on her clit, she expected the pleasure to diminish, but the lower speed pulse of vibration amplified the sensation of the inner beads. A slow grin spread over Zack's face as her breaths huffed quickly in and out.

"Slicken your clit and press harder." He watched her obey and then ordered, "Twitch those legs together slowly and then widened them as far as they'll go."

As she followed his directions, he slowly increased the power on the inner beads. "Now rub that clit hard enough to give me your pleasure and let me hear you come."

Those inner beads raced up and down within the toy as her finger glided over her clit. The ball gag muffled her long wail as the first waves of bliss tore through her, but the primal lust in Zack's gaze saturated her mind and gave her the first taste of how dominating he could be. Then he swiftly stood so fast that her eyes failed to remain in contact. His exposed cock came into view, locking down her gaze with concrete force. The dildo died, reminding her that she'd just disobeyed him. She whimpered and looked up at him.

He shook his head and placed the remote down on the seat. Without a word, he removed the vibrator but left the ball gag and didn't release her from the chair. Then he began to stroke his cock while keeping eye contact with her, but his expression showed no pleasure. Inches from her face, the movement of his hand squeezing and working his cock could only mean one thing. She'd barely realized it when his warm cum splattered across her face.

"That's what wasted pleasure feels like, love. Let's go shower for now. Tomorrow, you'll obey me, and we won't waste our pleasure again. Agree?"

"Mmm-hmm," she grunted, fully understanding his point and trying to hide her disappointment. But he'd tricked her!

Damn you, I'll be ready for anything you dish out tomorrow, she thought as he unstrapped her from the chair and removed her ball gag. Showered and exhausted, her last thought, like a mantra, before sleep was *anything he says, I'll be ready!*

But tomorrow would prove to test her readiness in more ways that she could ever imagine. After a restful night curled in Zack's arms, she awoke to hear him in the kitchen. The aroma of coffee assaulted her as she rolled out of bed. Zack had her cell phone on the table and, as she entered, told her, "He's emailed you twice."

Gwen checked her email and then looked over to see that it was seventeen minutes after seven. The email wanted them to meet Don at a hotel around an hour away.

"The meeting is scheduled at nine-thirty, so we have time to eat." She handed her phone to Zack and asked, "Do you know where that is?"

"Let's see." His finger swiped over her screen, and then he shrugged. "I don't have a clue, but my GPS does."

She rolled her eyes as she took her phone. They settled down for a quick breakfast before she hurried to gather what she needed. They set off and arrived a little early. Completely excited, Gwen hugged Don and said, "This is just what I needed."

"Your career, too," Don told her. "I was shocked when they requested you, but I have to admit it's brilliant."

He shook Zack's hand and apologized up front. "I'm sorry, but you are going to be so damn bored. Most of it will be makeup, cameras rolling which means they'll sew your lips shut if you make any noise, and dealing with issues."

Zack shrugged. "Gotta do what I gotta do, I guess. Do they have any security around?"

Don pointed out a man dressed in all black who was posted at the door. "Hotel security, but they did say they'd cover costs for any extra which should be arriving any minute."

"I might step out for lunch or to take a walk now and then but I won't go far," Zack told Gwen while looking around.

"Okay." She nodded as Don added, "So far, they seem to run things pretty efficiently so I don't think we have anything to worry about. Besides, she'll be tucked away in a conference room where no one but the crews will see her." He glanced at his watch and said, "The makeup crew had just arrived before you did. Zack, do you want to join us? This may take a couple of hours."

"A *couple of hours*?! For makeup?"

Gwen explained, "The makeup will be seen under harsh lights and making me look different takes longer."

"Okay," Zack said and warned her, "Keep your phone nearby. If you don't see me around, call me once every hour or so. If I don't hear from you, I'll be showing up with the police so don't forget."

"I'll remind her," Don assured him.

Zack didn't kiss her in public, but his eyes said enough. He retraced his steps and looked around for a place to wait. Inside, Gwen followed Don to the elevator which took them to the fourth floor. She asked him about their plans to change her appearance, but he didn't know much.

"From what I can tell, everything is hush-hush. I figured, as your agent, I'd have a right to know about makeup, but..."

He opened the conference room and a hand reached out and pulled her inside at the same time that Don pushed her from behind. Gwen didn't have the chance to utter a sound before something was placed over her mouth and nose. She tried to fight but froze when a light turned on across the room to show a face, identical to Gwen's, staring at her from a mirror.

"Hello, Gwen," the woman said. "Relax. We're here to alter your appearance."

The rag over her mouth muffled her shriek when a burning invaded her muscles. She slumped in Don's arms and her purse slid to the floor. She awoke to sore muscles, but at a failed attempt to move her arm, Gwen fought to drag herself from the depths of intense drowsiness. A male voice said her name and, thinking it was Zack, she tried to tell him something. A gag stopped her.

Her eyelids fluttered open to a blinding light while her mind flitted this way and that, unable to form but one cohesive thought.

"Phone…where's…my phone…"

Everything blurred before darkness swept over her again. The next time she awoke, Wren was staring down at her with an odd expression.

"Almost there, sis," she said and grinned. "My home sweet home." A giggle escaped her. "I mean *your* home sweet home."

"Down in back!" a man snapped from the front seat.

In Gwen's drugged state, recognition of Don's voice took a moment. Wren slid down in the seat and put a finger to her lips. "Shhh! He can be as mean as a gator."

Gwen's eyes fluttered closed once again. Her last thought before sleep closed in was *Dad was right. She really is crazy!*

She awoke from being slapped hard across the face. Gwen tried to kick out, but her feet were secured to the legs of a chair.

"Hit her harder. If they arrive here, she can't be able to talk," a woman's voice said before a stinging blow wrenched her head to the left and blinding pain tore through her jaw.

Her cheek was now swelling and tears saturated the blindfold, but Gwen had already passed out.

"Remove her bindings and drag her over to the mattress," Don told Wren. "Then, I'll drag what's-his-face in here, and we'll leave before the cops surround this

181

place." Don bent to kiss her but stopped at the last moment and smiled. "No one will ever guess you're not the real Gwen."

Wren nodded. "You bet your ass they won't."

"My ass isn't the one guaranteeing us a bank roll," he chuckled and shook his head. "We should have done this years ago."

They quickly worked together to remove the ropes binding Gwen to the chair, then dragged her over to the mattress. Next, they dragged one of the male models who they'd paid to pose as a Dom with Wren and placed him next to Gwen.

Hurrying out to Don's SUV, he urged Wren to tell him what she'd tell the police when they were inevitably pulled over.

"I'll show them Gwen's ID, let them know that you and I escaped from her *crazy* sister's clutches after a knock-down drag-out fight, and tell them where she and her Dom are hiding out."

"Brace yourself," was the only warning Don gave her before he slapped her hard. She stumbled backward and took a minute for the world to stop spinning. She gave him no warning at all before her fist collided with his jaw. After a few more well-placed punches, the two were satisfied and climbed into the SUV to head out.

Don quickly accelerated over the posted speed limit as he smiled, distancing them from the two future jailbirds. Don expected to be the *hero* for rescuing 'Gwen.' She'd stay with the PI for a short while, and then she'd choose her career over him. The PI could take his broken heart and shove it. She would reunite with Don to make bank on videos which had already been ordered. They'd only traveled three miles from the seemingly vacant building where they'd left Gwen, but both held complete confidence in their plans.

"Get those lips over here and give your agent a kiss," Don ordered her.

She unbuckled her seat belt and leaned sideways to obey him when a barely discernible thump sounded. Don immediately lost control of the vehicle. Their world turned into a blender of motion. The airbags deployed, but the driver's seat back tore loose and sent Don toppling backwards. His head slammed multiple locations before he crashed through the back windshield. Wren had been thrown through the front windshield shortly after he'd lost control. She smashed into a tree which broke her neck on impact.

Gwen awoke hours later and didn't trust her eyes. Was that Zack or was she hallucinating? When Vic came into view, she tried to speak, but pain blasted through her head.

"Don't try to talk, love. Your jaw is wired shut." He was frowning down at her with regret filling his eyes. "You're in the hospital. I'll explain everything later. Just rest for now."

Gwen raised her arm and winced before exhaustion set in. When she came to again, Zack was still there and talking in hushed tones with her father. She moaned and managed to point to a pad of paper. When he handed it over, she scrawled out, "Hi, Dad. What happened?"

"Honey, the doctor will be in to see you shortly, and I can't say much until he gives the go ahead," her dad explained.

"Love, you're doing great, but like your dad says, the doctor has to okay some things before you stress out over details," Zack explained and then slid a clipboard forward. "Can you sign this so the doctor is allowed to freely talk to me about your progress?" Zack asked, and watched her slowly apply her signature to the release form.

After that one signature, she was too exhausted to write anything more down. When she fell asleep again, Zack turned the paper in at the nurse's station, requesting a copy for his records. He'd pestered the doctor for a day and a half for information only to get blessed out by Gwen's mother who caused a scene over every damn thing she could. He'd gotten an update on Gwen's condition from her father. Everyone with the slightest bit of common sense now kept quiet about her father visiting. Her mother hadn't even stepped foot in Gwen's room, yet she'd made a point of terrorizing nurses and doctors.

On the fourth day in the hospital, Gwen was awake and feeling better. The doctor was now standing in her room and studying her as Vic and Zack answered her questions. She'd just written, "Explain."

"Don and Wren had found a few lesser-known and ill-reputed places that placed orders for future videos. They were equipped to take custom orders for sex tapes, namely anything anyone wanted no matter what or how bad it was, so they planned to switch you and Wren. You would spend time in prison for Wren's involvement in the murder of a male model while Wren would rake in money by acting demure and wearing your name."

Gwen held the notepad up to show them. "How did you find me?"

"You know that app I loaded on your phone?" Zack asked and, when she nodded, he told her, "Vic had already programmed a tiny device that looks like a nail which I pushed into the collar of your blouse before you left. It tracked your location and stored audio of what was said anywhere around you."

She held up the tablet again. "Tell me what happened to them."

Vic and Zack looked at each other, but the doctor answered for them. "They hit a police spike strip at high speed and went airborne. The outcome was fatal. You are now safe, Gwen."

Both Vic and Zack agreed and thanked the doctor, who nodded politely. He started out the door but ducked back in at the last moment. He looked from her to Zack and announced, "We have problems. *She's* here."

Frowning, Gwen tried to make out what he meant but understood when she heard her mother's voice. She snatched the notepad up and pointed frantically at the door, then signaled to let her in.

Zack stepped beside the bed, ready to tackle their new brand of evil if and when it walked through the door. Gwen's hand wrapped around his arm, as she made a negative sound and pulled to move him out of her way.

"You say the…um, write the word, and she will be banned from this room," the doctor informed her. "And I can guarantee you'll have a floor full of personnel who will forever remember your act of kindness."

The door was flung open, and her mother stomped into the room. Her sour expression rapidly turned to surprise when Gwen launched the notebook at her face, followed by everything within her reach.

Thanks so much for reading this book, The Dominant Detective and Slandered Submissive! To hear about more of my books, and to get a free story, sign up

for my e-mail list at
www.kumquatpublishing.com/alexandra
If you enjoyed this book then I'd love for
you to leave a review on its Amazon
page!

Also by Alexandra Noir:

High Tide

He came to the beach every day, his ebony body a vision of sculpted perfection befitting a Nubian prince. His hair was close-cropped to his skull, his sculpted muscles rippling in sensual rhythm with each movement. Approaching the shore on a small, brightly painted motorboat, he dragged the boat onto the pristine, sugar-white sand and hauled out a net bag bulging with shells.

Today he wore loose, turquoise-blue swim shorts that matched the calm, mirror-brilliance of the ocean and more than emphasized his generous bulge. As was his habit, he hefted the bag of shells over his shoulder and walked east.

Swinging lazily on a hammock stretched between two arched coconut palms, Kendra watched the man from beneath the wide brim of her straw hat. Early each morning, she heard the muted thrum of the boat long before it appeared where the cerulean sky merged with the crystalline water. The speck steadily approached the secluded beach peppered with palms trees and a scattering of upscale residences.

The community was exclusive, the residents paying a premium to enjoy a private paradise. Some were retired, others were artistic types who found inspiration in the idyllic environment. Some, like Kendra and Josh, were into a more nomadic lifestyle that allowed them the freedom to do what they wanted, when they wanted, and with whom they wanted.

Both had decided early in their marriage that traditional roles and relationships held no interest for them. The only child of eccentric archeologists, Kendra was used to traveling the world and spending time at exotic digs. She'd followed in her parents' footsteps by earning a degree in archeology, and had met Josh on a dig in Egypt.

Tall, bronzed, with sun-bleached blond hair, Josh was an easygoing, affable Egyptologist obsessed with the ancient culture. He too was an only child, his parents a British diplomat and a renowned pianist. He'd developed his passion for Egypt when his father was attached to the Cairo embassy throughout most of Josh's childhood. Though his father was transferred to the embassy in Athens when Josh entered university, Josh remained in Cairo to finish his studies.

It was five years after graduation that he met Kendra on a dig in Thebes. The attraction was instantaneous, and Josh's golden looks starkly contrasted Kendra's creamy, freckled complexion, mellow amber eyes, and shock of carrot-red hair. Josh had the slim physique of a runner, while Kendra's softy curvaceous figure mimicked that of a ripe pear. While Josh tanned easily, Kendra had to constantly avoid getting sunburnt in the unforgiving climate.

Something about the desert heat always left Kendra in a perpetual state of arousal, and she found herself masturbating whenever she had the opportunity. A precocious child, she had discovered a voracious appetite for sex at an early age, and was reading about the erotic frescoes of Pompeii when other children were still playing with toys. Her parents were open-minded, and encouraged both her curiosity and intelligence. It was no surprise that she started university at sixteen and began apprenticing with her parents after graduating with honors.

Kendra traveled with her parents around the world until they finally became semi-permanent residents of Egypt. Far from civilization, embraced by the lingering spirit of an ancient culture, she particularly enjoyed sleeping naked in a tent, the flap opened to the stars. Spreading herself open on her hands and knees, she slowly fondled her body, paying particular attention to her generous breasts, before trailing her fingers to her pussy and ass both saturated by the juice leaking from her pussy.

She was fond of edging, which brought her to the verge of coming until she was trembling, aching, and drenched in sweat. Sometimes it took only a fleeting touch to elicit a shattering orgasm, but to prolong her pleasure, she often fucked herself with the rounded handle of her hairbrush by thrusting it deeply inside her pussy, imagining that it was a thick cock pounding her.

If she was feeling particularly hungry, she also slid the juice-slicked handle into her ass. That she did this in front of the open flap only added to intensity when she came. She liked to imagine phantom eyes watching and exploring her body with her. But it provided only temporary relief, and she was constantly plagued with a heavy, sensual languor that begged for release.

When Josh arrived at the dig, it was as though her prayers had been answered. Not only did they work well together, but Kendra's parents loved him. If they noticed the chemistry between Josh and their daughter, they made no effort to thwart the relationship, and their long hours at various digs provided Kendra and Josh ample opportunity to be alone.

One afternoon while supervising a smaller dig with only assistants and workers, Kendra and Josh took off ostensibly to pick up supplies from the primary dig. On the way, they stopped at a remote oasis and parked the Range Rover in the midst of a dense cluster of date palms. Shaded from view, they spread a blanket on the sand and fucked like a pair of starving animals.

It was quick and hard. Kendra had mounted Josh in a sixty-nine position, her approving gaze fixed on his thick cock. It rose like a fleshy obelisk that vanished into her mouth an inch at a time. Gripping the base of his cock with one hand, she caressed his balls with the other, pausing occasionally to lick and suck them. She enjoyed feeling them tighten in her mouth, the taut skin the texture of an orange peel.

Josh's tongue and fingers spread her pussy across his face and explored her juicy, pink folds. His teasing nibbles on her riding clit caused her to furiously grind against his mouth. When his tongue began to snake inside her at the same time his slick fingers slithered into her ass, Kendra jerked so violently against his face that he had to push her off before she suffocated him.

Unable to keep from busting all over Kendra's face, Josh got up, pushed Kendra onto her knees, grabbed her hips, and impaled her on his cock. His grip was so tight his fingers left imprints on her flesh. He drove himself deep inside her and violently thrust. Kendra's full breasts swung like pendulums, her face pressed close to the blanket.

Their cries rose above the hot, breathless silence. Between the dense palm fronds, the steel-blue sky merged into the glare of the sun. Both came quickly and explosively. For Kendra, it was the most intense orgasm she'd ever experienced. She felt as though she'd been turned inside out, and every cell, every pore, resonated from the energy.

Gasping for breath, their bodies slick with sweat, they collapsed into each others' arms and lay on the blanket. For a moment, time seemed suspended. Neither spoke as they absorbed the ancient spirit that seemed to flow with the shimmering heat waves. There was a history here, a legacy of time that made Kendra feel more than naked, but exposed in body and soul.

It was only when they rose to dress that they noticed a pair of camels plodding away over a nearby dune, their swathed riders turned away. Neither Kendra nor Josh said a word as their silent audience vanished from sight, but both had thought the same.

They had been turned on by being watched. The encounter was clearly random. The oasis was a well-known stopping point for travelers, but in all the times Kendra had visited the oasis, she'd never seen anyone. Yet the thought of faceless strangers watching her get fucked aroused both she and Josh so much that they fell once again onto the blanket.

His cock was already a truncheon, hard and hungry. This time Kendra straddled him and rode him, her juice slurping as she bounced hard on him, hands digging into his shoulders. Josh caressed her swinging breasts and tweaked her rigid nipples before pulling them into his mouth. Kendra yelped when he circled them with his tongue and nibbled them with his teeth.

By now Kendra's hair was a tangled, sweaty mess, and she smelled her sweat and the musk of her sex. Her orgasm exploded from her core and erupted with volcanic intensity. She thrust her head back and screamed, her primal cry absorbed by the heat. Josh had to push off her hands to keep her long nails from drawing blood. He jizzed so much and so deeply inside her that it gushed from her pussy when she slipped off of him.

When they finally collapsed onto the blanket, they could barely keep their eyes open. Though it was tempting to take a nap, they knew they had to get moving soon. Josh lazily twirled a strand of Kendra's hair.

"We should get going before it gets too late," he said. "After all, weren't we supposed to pick up some supplies?"

Kendra laughed and got to her feet.

"Wouldn't it be funny if we met our mysterious voyeurs at the market?"

Josh grinned and reached for his clothes.

"Wouldn't it be funny if they were workers at the dig?"

They shared a laugh and climbed into the Rover to continue their journey. A year later they married, and their interest in archeological exploration segued into an exploration of their sexuality that eventually evolved into a passion for exhibitionist sex in primarily outdoor locations. Admittedly, there had been a few close calls, but neither could deny that it kept their relationship alive while those of many of their friends and colleagues ended in separation or divorce.

***

Smiling at the memory, Kendra sipped on her customary morning pineapple mojito. She and Josh had certainly traveled a unique journey together. The drink's frosty coolness soothed the heat that infused her body from more than the balmy temperature. Apart from the gentle susurration of the water and the squawk of parrots, nothing disturbed the serenity of the morning.

Though she and Josh had been coming to their secluded Caribbean island retreat for several years, she'd never noticed the man until two weeks ago. She and Josh had spent most of their time relaxing or swimming, the hectic days of sightseeing long relegated to their first year on the island. The tiny jewel offered the beauty and benefits of the larger islands without the crowds or congestion. They had what they needed, and the simplicity of their lives suited them.

The first time Kendra saw the man, she'd been dozing on the hammock. She often got up early to watch the sunrise, but over time it became a habit and sometimes she even spent the night on the hammock. Such was the freedom that she and Josh enjoyed on the island.

Hearing the faint thrum of a motor, Kendra had gazed at the sea and noticed a moving speck that gradually became a small boat. Boldly decorated with parrot-bright colors, it was unlike any other boat

Kendra had seen around the island. She watched curiously as the man switched off the motor and carefully beached the boat.

It wasn't until he reached for a net bag stuffed with a variety of gorgeous shells that she noticed how equally gorgeous he was. Perhaps early thirties, his lithe, panther-like body moved with a liquidity that defied gravity. But it was his face that instantly attracted Kendra. High cheekbones, full, sensual lips, a strong jawline...the only detail she couldn't quite determine was the color of his eyes.

Her gaze had fallen to prominent bulge on his teal board shorts. Taking another sip of her mojito to quench at least one thirst, she imagined what his gleaming, ebony cock would look like. He was big, at least seven inches, and probably quite thick, though it looked as if he had the balls of a stallion as well.

An intense sexual thrill coursed through her body. She could almost feel the man's strong hands spreading her thighs and thrusting that meaty cock deep inside her wet pussy, stretching her as he filled her. While Josh was a good size, she had yet to experience someone bigger even though they'd had their share of encounters with other men.

Since Kendra had expressed her desire to feel of another man's cock inside her a few years after their marriage, she and Josh had gradually filtered into arrangements where Josh would watch another man of their choosing fuck her. She was fascinated by men of different cultures, and was in search of the ultimate experience. This allowed Josh to not only indulge his voyeurism, but when he fucked Kendra afterward, the experience was mind-blowing for both.

Kendra smiled. She was glad that she wore her hat and sunglasses. At least she could admire the mysterious visitor without being obvious. If the man noticed her scrutiny, he gave no notice. She wondered why he would come to their stretch of beach since there was nothing commercial in the area, but when she noticed him walking east, she assumed he had a destination, probably one of the residences.

She was growing hungry. Usually she and Josh had breakfast on the patio, but she was curious about the man. Josh had stayed up late working on his memoirs, so he wouldn't be up for a while anyway. She settled against her cushion and continued to sip on her morning mojito.

About an hour later, the man returned, the empty net bag slung over his shoulder. He walked with a confident stride, as though he owned the beach. Kendra watched him approach the boat. He tossed in the bag and pushed the boat toward the gently rippling water, waded in until it floated free, and jumped inside. Kendra noticed how the water gleamed on his skin. The motor coughed to life. The man steered out to sea and turned westward.

Now, two weeks later, Kendra watched a routine that could have been timed to the minute. After the man headed east, she dozed for almost an hour, and then woke a couple of minutes before he returned. As always, the empty net was slung over his shoulder. He approached the boat and started pushing it toward the water.

Suddenly, he stopped and looked directly at Kendra. His gaze was so intense, so direct, she felt as though he could see her eyes through her sunglasses. Shocked by his scrutiny, Kendra froze. He'd never noticed, or at least, acknowledged her before. What had changed now? Something about his face suggested he was smiling. He stared at her for a few moments.

Kendra was so entranced by his gaze that she only glimpsed the motion of his hand. She blinked. Had he just touched his cock? It was only a flicker of motion from her peripheral vision, so she couldn't be sure. Then he touched it again, though this time it was a slower, deliberate stroke. Kendra didn't need binoculars to envision his growing bulge. Even from a distance it was noticeable.

Snared by the hypnotic motion of his hands, Kendra felt herself growing wet. She stared hungrily at the man, her imagination running wild with erotic images of the two entangled in the sand. Her hand drifted to the top of her sundress and pulled it down to reveal her breasts. Looking at the man, she tweaked her already rigid nipples, and paused to raise one breast to her mouth and suck.

The man watched entranced. By now his cock was rigid, and rose from his shorts like a flagpole. Kendra stared at it, willing the man to expose his proud meat. The man seemed to smile. Perhaps he could read her thoughts? He watched her for a few moments, hesitated, and finally turned to the boat and pushed it onto the water.

Kendra could only stare as the motor kicked in and the boat moved away from the beach. He glanced back only once before the boat gradually vanished into the western horizon.

"Like the show?" Josh asked, touching her shoulder.

Kendra started. She'd been so focused on the man she never heard Josh approach. He grinned at her and bent to kiss her.

"When did you get up?" she asked, pulling him onto the hammock.

"Little while ago," he said, gazing out to sea. "Thought I'd bring out breakfast, but I see you've already decided on a man course."

Kendra snuggled against him. Josh's hands strayed to her breasts. He fondled and kissed them, bringing each to his mouth to suck her nipples. Kendra sighed and leaned back against the cushion as Josh's hand strayed between her legs and pushed her thighs apart.

"Too bad he left," Josh said, toying with her pussy lips. "Maybe we could have put on a little show for him."

\Kendra writhed and spread her legs wider apart. Josh toyed with her swollen clit, causing her to jerk and gasp. Sliding his fingers deep into her wetness, Josh teased her G-spot until she came, her body shuddering from the intense release.

"Feel better?" he asked.

Kendra nodded and stretched languorously.

"You've seen him?" she asked.

"Of course I've noticed him. He's impossible to miss. And I have to admit I'm also curious about him. Maybe we could both greet him tomorrow."

Kendra chuckled. "He may not want to leave."

Josh grinned and kissed her. "Maybe he can take something else with him besides an empty bag." He paused to gaze at the horizon. "Weather report this morning says that Hurricane Brett's picking up steam."

"I thought it was steering north of us?"

"It's changed direction, which they often do. We might be in its path, or at least the north side of the island."

Kendra sat up. "Are we in danger?"

"We've weathered other storms," Josh said, "but this one's pretty big. Could do some damage. We may have to wait it out in the shelter, but no one's sure yet which way it's going to turn."

Kendra frowned. One of few disadvantages to living in the Caribbean was hurricanes. They'd chosen the southern coast of the island for a reason, as historically, storms tended to strike the northern coast. Even though they'd dealt with severe weather in the past, it was never enough to threaten their home. However, they opted for prudence by building a shelter below ground and reinforcing their home as much as possible.

"Is it that bad?" she asked.

"Could be. Season so far has been a record-breaker."

"Is there anything we need?" Kendra asked. "Just in case…"

Josh rose and stretched. He wore his favorite tropical print board shorts. Even after twenty years of marriage, he was as buff and handsome as the day they met. She knew that in his eyes, she'd barely changed, although her figure had grown more voluptuous with age and her eyes creased delightfully when she smiled.

"We should be good, but I'll check everything to make sure we're prepared."

"I'll make breakfast," Kendra said, stepping out of the hammock and following him to the house.

Gazing at the lush foliage surrounding their cozy beach house, she felt a pang of concern. Approaching the open patio doors, she turned to look back at the calm sea. A sailboat skipped across the horizon. The day was so beautiful, the fragrant air so balmy, the only sound the gentle susurration of the water and the chatter of birds. It was difficult to imagine that how quickly the idyllic view could change into one of violent, raging waters and destructive winds.

Kendra felt a knot of concern churn in her stomach. As she entered the house, she wondered what the next day would bring.

About Alexandra Noir

Alexandra Noir is a registered relationship counselor and social worker. She's always had dirty fantasies locked inside of her mind and now loves writing about them and occasionally experiencing them. Her free time often consists of BDSM play where she submits to men that can bring her to places most women only dream of. Every so often though, she finds herself on the other side of the flogger and can bring a man to his knees.

She writes about BDSM, kink, and power exchange.

Free Story!

You can join her email list at http://www.kumquatpublishing.com/alexandra/ and get a free story! You'll also hear about new books as they become available and how to get some books for free!

Printed in Great Britain
by Amazon

60967196R00122